Kose Ventures LLC

Library of Congress Control Number: 2021916158

Published by Rowland Publishing, Inc. in Tallahassee, Florida

Cover Illustration by Lainey Rothschild

THE
COLSON LEGEND
ICE QUEEN

BY MICHAEL NYIKOS

In the year 2001, a billionaire by the name of Austen Wolfe created a secret group called the Strings on All Society, also known as S.O.A.S. The group originally consisted of the world's richest and deadliest people with the goal of achieving a society governed by them. They wanted people to be under their control so that no individual would have the free will to make a decision on their own. They have been able to hide this secret from the public in order to control the world through the shadows. In the present time, Austen Wolfe's operation has grown immensely. Given the group's large supply of money, they are on the verge of controlling everyone like puppets. Austen Wolfe and the rest of the S.O.A.S. will do anything to maintain their control over the population—even if it requires doing a task that is less than lawful.

Over the years that the S.O.A.S. has existed, they have feared the four Farisphonites. The Farisphonites are the living conscience that inhabit each of the four stones. These special beings have vowed to protect the stones from being destroyed at all costs by wielding their special powers. The urban legend of the Power of Four states that an alien by the name of Hapto was traveling deep into space right around the time of the Big Bang. Once the Big Bang occurred, his ship was destroyed in seconds, and Hapto's body disintegrated into particles the size of sand. However, Hapto's heart was made from a type of alien technology that the Big Bang was not able to disintegrate. Therefore, Hapto's heart was still intact and was smashed into four pieces taking the form of stones: the earth stone, the red stone, the ice gem, and the death stone. These stones each possess unique abilities and serve as a leach to people with compatible bloodlines. If a person or group of people are able to destroy all four stones, then that person or group will gain the powers that each stone possesses which will enable him to use those powers to control society itself. These stones are a great threat to the S.O.A.S. because if he is unable to destroy all four stones, then the Farisphonites will be able to use their powers against him. Because of this, Austen Wolfe has been on high alert to find these stones and destroy all four in order to achieve his ultimate goal.

In the current time of 2020, Austen Wolfe has managed to destroy the earth stone and the red stone. However, two stones still remain in some part of the world, and they are the only possible hope of stopping Austen Wolfe and the S.O.A.S.

CHAPTER ONE

LIAM SCARR

I strutted up to the S.O.A.S. building wearing a brand-new black suit jacket and pants. Underneath my jacket, I wore a striking dark blue, button-down shirt with a black and blue striped tie. My short, spiky black hair was a little messy, just the way I like it. I pushed my hand through my hair as the automatic doors at the entrance to the building slid open. There were hundreds of people walking around the huge modernistic lobby.

"Mr. Scarr," the woman at the front desk announced as I walked toward her with a confused look on my face. "Mr. Wolfe would like to see you immediately," she said. I looked at her cynically. I knew exactly why Mr. Wolfe wanted to speak to me, and I knew it wasn't going to be a pleasant discussion.

"I'll get on that," I replied rudely as I headed toward the elevator.

I took the elevator to the top floor aware that my job at the company could be in jeopardy based on my actions the previous night. I walked through the large glass doors into a sizable waiting room. There were a few men in suits sitting on large, upholstered chairs reading the newspaper, but overall, the room was mostly empty. I stood in the center of the room trying to get anyone's attention who could help me find out where I was supposed to meet with Mr. Wolfe, but no one seemed to acknowledge me. It did not appear that anyone was in charge. I finally saw a few of the men look up from their newspapers and stare at me with dirty looks on their faces.

"Are you Liam Scarr?" one of the men said as he stood up out of his chair.

"Depends on who's asking," I said.

"The boss would like to speak with you," he replied as he pointed toward a large office branching off from the other side of the waiting room. I slowly walked to the door and pushed it open without knocking. Mr. Wolfe was sitting at his desk, and he immediately stood up when I walked in. He straightened his black suit jacket as he tossed his black tie on the floor of his office. He had on a red, button-down shirt underneath his suit jacket along with black shiny shoes that matched. His hair was a combination of brown and grey, which was clearly starting to turn all grey, and slicked back neatly. He stared at me intently.

"Mr. Scarr, nice of you to drop by," Mr. Wolfe said.

"I heard you wanted to see me," I replied.

"Yes, you know...I was very displeased with a phone call I

received late last night. Your assignment was to ensure that Bethany Anderson followed through with her wedding. However, it appears that Bethany Anderson broke her engagement and is now single again. She will not be getting married, and she and her fiancé will not be going on their honeymoon to Saint Martin as planned. I'm confused why that would be the case since you were supposed to ensure that the marriage took place," he said angrily.

"Her fiancé was abusive. The woman was terrified. It didn't feel like it was my choice to make," I replied. Mr. Wolfe reached into the bottom drawer of his desk as he pulled out an orbuculum.

"This orbuculum is far more advanced than any technology we have in the year 2020. It is able to give us a glimpse into the future. In the year 2025, the S.O.A.S. will have complete control over the population. We will have finally created a socialistic society with no free will. However, in order for this particular future to occur, we must make the necessary changes. Ensuring that Bethany Anderson got married was an event that needed to occur. Since that event ceases to exist, the possible future the orbuculum presented is now in jeopardy... because of you," he said sternly.

"Do you want me to say I'm sorry?" I asked snarkily.

"I didn't recruit an arrogant thief because I wanted to

make friends. I recruited you because I wanted someone to complete missions with the utmost skill without having any feelings toward a wife that gets beaten. I thought you weren't sentimental, but it seems as if I was wrong," he said as he signaled for the men to come into his office. Four large men quickly dispersed throughout Mr. Wolfe's office. They all looked at me with disgust.

"You're a loose cannon Liam. I can't have you interfering with my affairs any longer. Your time here has come to an end," he said. I looked around at the large men surrounding me.

"Congratulations," I replied. Mr. Wolfe signaled to the men as they slowly closed in on me.

"Take care of him," Mr. Wolfe said, smiling. The men dragged me out the back door and tossed me onto the concrete. They all circled around me as I laid on the ground. One of the men pulled out a Glock 22 and pointed it at me.

"We can't have any loose ends compromising our goal," the man with the gun said.

"I guess it's time to die then," I replied.

"I'm glad we are on the same page," he said. I slowly reached for my right ankle as I grabbed my black-and-white striped Desert Eagle pistol.

"Me too," I said as one bullet flew directly into the man's forehead. The man immediately dropped, and the other men looked at the dead man nervously. They reached into their pants for their pistols, but before they could do so, I shot two of them and pistol-whipped the other. I quickly scanned the back parking lot, and it was completely empty. I began to strut down the street away from the S.O.A.S. building hoping to leave my past behind.

Chapter Two

Jack Colson

My alarm sounded as the clock struck seven. I rolled over in my bed as I unplugged my alarm clock, which instantly stopped the ringing. I rubbed my face as I was still extremely tired and picked up my phone to scroll through my emails. There were hundreds of messages from colleges promoting their schools and encouraging students like me to apply. A lot of people have been asking me what I want to be when I grow up. My mom has been nagging me about this for a year, and I have yet to come up with an answer. I don't even know what I'm having for breakfast this morning, and she expects me to know what I want to do in five years. I haven't applied to any colleges, and my mom is concerned about it. Personally, I'm not interested in pursuing my education. I'm not book smart. I don't want to learn about physics, English, or any type of school subjects. I want to make a difference in the world and pursue my own path. I have always been considerate of others, and I intend to inspire social awareness.

My name is Jack Colson, and I'm an 18-year-old high school senior in Brookfield, Connecticut. I'm an only child, and all my life it has just been my mom and me. My father has been out of the picture since the day I was born. I never met him, and I don't intend to. My mom is constantly working long hours during the day at the law firm, and she spends the nights with her boyfriend Dale. He treats my mom well, so I don't hate him, but he never seems to acknowledge my existence. He barely hangs out with me and doesn't even attempt to go out of his way to talk to me. I spend most of my days hanging out with friends when I'm not at school. My best friend is Brian Shadow. I practically live at his house. The Shadows are like a second family to me. He's my closest friend, and I've known him for years. I met him in the fourth grade, and we've been hanging out ever since. We played sports together, we rode bikes together, and we went trick or treating together every Halloween.

Being a teenager changes things though, and now we mostly hang out in someone's basement with a rack of beer. Brian is extremely intelligent, and I was so proud of him when I heard that he got a full ride to Cornell University. He suggested that I enroll in Tompkins Cortland Community College because it's only fifteen minutes away from Cornell so we could room together. Honestly, I'm just not interested in following Brian to college. Besides, that's a lot of money being thrown down the drain for something I have no interest in pursuing.

"Jack, come downstairs," my mom called up to me.

"I'm coming!" I replied as I quickly threw on my clothes and rushed downstairs. I flew down the staircase and sprinted to the kitchen. My mom was standing there with two suitcases sitting at her feet.

"Jack honey, have you sent in any college applications yet?" she asked.

"Mom, I want to be honest with you. I don't want to go to college next year. I'm not that smart anyway, and I'd rather devote my life to making a difference in the world rather than achieving a diploma," I replied.

"Jack, I've always loved your dedication to helping others, but that isn't a job. Community service work and fundraising are important, but those aren't jobs honey," she said.

"I know, but it's my choice. I'll want to pursue an adventure of my own when I get older. I don't care about the money," I said.

"Whatever makes you happy," she replied.

"Where are you going?" I asked curiously.

"Dale is taking me to Saint Martin, so I'll be out of town for a couple of weeks. He was lucky to get tickets. There was a last-minute cancellation which was incredibly lucky," she replied.

Beep! Beep!

"Oh, that's him. I love you honey," she said as she gave me a kiss on the cheek.

"I love you, too," I replied as she grabbed her suitcases and ran out the door.

I've been doing tons of community service, and I've attended a few fundraisers. As I mentioned before, I want to go on my own adventure. I'm absurdly confused that it took me this long to realize what I want to do with my life. It sounds crazy, but I live in Brookfield where the streets are run by gangs, and everyone lives in fear. I just want to escape this dangerous town. It's only a matter of time. Coincidently, the dream I had last night aided my decision. It was strange because this dream didn't feel like an ordinary dream. It felt different. It's hard to explain, but it almost felt like it happened or was destined to happen. I don't exactly know, but there was this mysterious girl. I didn't see her face, but she was dressed in all black and seemed to know me pretty well.

When I got to school, I walked through the doors of the classroom and headed to the back of the room. Brian was sitting at a lab table by himself, and he signaled for me to come over. Brian had on khaki pants with a grey, quarter-zip pullover. His short brown hair was neatly combed to the right, and he was wearing his black glasses. He was dressed pretty nerdy if you ask me, but that's how he normally dressed. I was wearing jeans and a dark grey sweatshirt, which I considered to be a pretty cool outfit. Unlike Brian, I don't wear glasses, and my long brown hair was wavy and a little messy, which is how I liked it.

Ding, ding, ding.

"Okay class, take your seats. We have much to discuss in such a short amount of time," Ms. Montgomery said anxiously as she immediately walked to the blackboard and began scribbling down notes.

"Yo, Jack," someone whispered. I looked over, and it was Dylan. Dylan is also one of my closest friends. He was dressed pretty cool with his jeans and his plain white, long-sleeve shirt. He definitely is not nerdy like Brian. He looks very similar to me except for the fact that he has blonde hair. He was sitting at the lab table directly next to Brian and me.

"What's up?" I whispered.

"Hopefully, Montgomery doesn't lash out at you again for zoning out. I thought it was funny, but I still hate her. She's such a hardo," he said.

"I don't know what she expects. I can't listen to that woman talk for forty minutes. It's painfully boring," I replied.

"Hahahaha, I know, right?" Dylan responded. I pulled out my notebook and began doodling on the side of the paper. I shaped the outline of a man holding a shield in his hand.

I shaded in the shield with my pencil and drew a star in the middle. I then sketched that same star on the man's chest and on the mask he had covering his face. I was trying to draw Steve Rogers, aka Captain America, but it didn't really look too much like him.

"Can anyone tell me what the formula for Newton's second law is?" Ms. Montgomery asked the class. I saw Brian out of the corner of my eye raising his hand and shaking with excitement. I didn't even look up to acknowledge her question. I just continued scribbling in my notebook attempting to draw a better Captain America.

"Mr. Colson," she said. The class all stared at me as I looked around confused.

"What was the question?" I replied. I looked on the board at some of her notes, but it may as well have been written in Spanish because I barely understood any of it.

"The question was what is Newton's second law. If you were listening to the lecture, you'd know. We just discussed it," she said. I knew that Ms. Montgomery was about to be very disappointed that I did not have any clue what Newton's second law was, nor did I even know there was a first law.

"Well?" she said rudely.

"I'm not sure," I replied.

"Is there anyone who would like to inform Mr. Colson what

Newton's second law is?" she asked. Brian's hand shot up like a rocket as he almost was jumping out of his seat to get Ms. Montgomery's attention.

"Mr. Shadow," she said.

"Newton's second law states that the net force of an object is equal to the mass of the object times its acceleration," Brian said proudly.

"That is correct," Ms. Montgomery replied, smiling.

"Once again Einstein," I whispered in Brian's ear.

"Jack, if you just listen rather than doodling during the whole class, you'd know this stuff. It's not that difficult," he said.

"Yeah, you're probably right, but the teacher already hates me and I'm not trying to be a physicist, so I think I'm good with not listening to her lecture," I replied. Brian just shook his head and then proceeded to write down every word written on the blackboard.

Ding, ding, ding.

"Okay class, remember that your next homework assignment is due on Monday. I hope everyone has a good weekend," she said. I packed up my notebook and threw it in my backpack. Dylan, Brian, and I all tossed our backpacks over our shoulders and headed toward the door.

"Oh, Mr. Colson, may I have a word with you?" she said.

Brian and Dylan both looked at me with their eyes wide open giving me the indication that I'm definitely in some sort of trouble.

"Good luck. We'll meet you outside," Dylan said as he patted me on the back. Dylan and Brian walked out of the class as I headed toward the front of the room.

"Jack, I'm concerned about your grade in this class. I didn't want to call you out again today, but it's a little difficult for me to watch you sit in the back of the classroom and just draw doodles of Captain America all during class. You're on track to fail this class if you don't put in some more effort," she said.

"I don't want to offend you, but I just don't see the point of listening to your class. I don't want to be a physicist when I'm older," I replied.

"So, what…do you think you're going to be the next Captain America? Jack, it's time to get a reality check. You need to start thinking about your future after high school and less about comic book heroes," she said.

"Okay, I will. I'll look into it over the weekend," I said even though I was well aware that I was lying.

"Have a good weekend," she said.

"You too," I replied as I quickly made my way out into the hallway.

I walked out of the school and headed toward Dylan and

Brian who were standing in the parking lot on the other side of the school.

"The senior trip?" Brian asked.

"Yeah, get this. No parents, boozing hard with the boys and tons of chicks; it's gonna be lit. Senior trip to Bermuda. Literally everyone is going. It's perfect since the drinking age is 18. We're all the legal age to drink," Dylan replied.

"That sounds awesome. That'd be a great way to forget about the whole college application process," I said.

"Yeah, we are all definitely going," Dylan replied.

"I am not going. This whole senior trip can destroy my whole academic career. One picture on Instagram with me holding a beer, and my scholarship would be revoked in an instant. My life would be over. I can't take that risk," Brian said nervously.

"Don't be like this. Nothing is going to happen. We're just going to have some drinks. The entire senior class is going. You can't be the only person to not go," Dylan said.

"Come on Brian. Think of it as a reward for all the hard work you've done. You got into Cornell. We are all graduating. It's our celebration of becoming men," I said.

"I guess it would be fun, but if any of you idiots even think of doing something that could jeopardize my scholarship in any way..."

"We won't," I said, cutting him off.

"And besides, what's the worst thing that could happen?" Dylan replied.

Chapter Three

Jack Colson

Brian, Dylan, and I quickly exited the tour bus as we stood in front of a magnificent hotel. All the students quickly clustered into the lobby after grabbing their luggage from the bus. The hotel lobby was enormous, consisting of hundreds of large, double-paned windows overlooking the ocean. There were multicolored couches with small tables adorned with an elaborate array of fruit bowls and flower arrangements. The teachers walked over to the front desk where they were handed multiple room keys which they proceeded to pass out to all of the students.

After a few minutes with our keys in our hands, we all took the elevator up to room 420. Since the rooms were only for two people, Brian had to stay in the room next door to Dylan and me. The room was beautifully decorated with white curtains and a large picture window which enabled us to have the most amazing view of the ocean. There were two twin beds, a television, a fridge, and a decent size bathroom. The normal components of a hotel room.

"This place is awesome," Dylan said as he pulled open the

curtain admiring the view. I heard a knock on the door, and I quickly jogged over to the door and flung it open to see Brian standing there.

"Brian how sick is this place?" Dylan said, still admiring the room.

"Yeah, you have a great set-up here," he replied.

"It's good you got the room next door," I said.

"Yeah, it's pretty convenient," he said as he pulled out the school's agenda for the trip.

"So it says on the agenda that we need to meet in the lobby in fifteen minutes for the tour of the Crystal and Fantasy Caves."

"I'll tell you right now. I'm not going to some stupid cave. We're on vacation. I'm hitting up the bar, and tonight we're going to this party on the beach," Dylan said as he pulled out a flyer for a tiki party tonight at eight.

"We are not attending some beach party tonight. Are you asking to get in trouble?" Brian said concerned.

"Hey, whoa whoa, Brian. Relax. Listen...you and I will go on the tour of the Crystal and Fantasy Caves while Dylan stays here. Later, we'll see what seems like the best place to go, and we'll go there," I said.

"Alright, but I told you guys I don't want to get in trouble," he replied as he started to walk out of the room. Dylan slowly walked over to me. I could feel him breathing on me as he tried to move swiftly so Brian wouldn't turn around and notice him.

"You were just telling him that right?" he whispered.

"Yeah, we're definitely going to that party."

"Let's go," he replied enthusiastically as I followed Brian out of the room.

The elevator doors shut as we slowly moved underground. A minute or two went by, and the doors slid open.

"Hello Brookfield High School Seniors. Welcome to the Crystal and Fantasy Caves," she said, or at least that's as much as I heard before I stopped listening. Brian looked intrigued in what she had to say, but I thought it was rather boring. She walked the students and faculty down a long narrow pathway. There were rocks that looked like large icicles hanging above us. The cave had minimal amounts of light, which made it difficult to see the gigantic rocks around me.

"This is amazing, isn't it?" Brian asked.

"Yeah. It's interesting," I replied sarcastically. I watched as Brian attempted to make his way to the front of the crowd, and I lost sight of where he went. I didn't want to listen to the tour guide ramble on about the history of the cave, or whatever she was saying, so I began to walk slower. Not too slow but slow enough that I would be passed by the other students. It took about a minute for me to reach the back of the crowd, which was great for me because I couldn't even hear the tour guide from here. I felt my leg vibrate from my phone. I reached into my pocket and found that Dylan had texted me.

"How's the tour?" he asked.

"Extremely boring. Brian's so invested in it, and I'm just standing at the back of the group not even listening."

"Hahahaha jokes," he replied quickly. I smiled as I chuckled at his text.

"Jack," someone said. I looked up, but no one appeared to be acknowledging me. I turned around and nobody was behind me. I glanced both ways, and I thought it was strange that no one was looking at me.

"Jack," the voice said again. I immediately came to a halt as I realized that the voice had come from behind me. However, there was no one standing there. The group had moved on without even noticing the fact that I had stopped. I had not realized until right now that there was a fork in the path behind me. One path led back to the entrance specifically where we just came from. That way was lit up with some lights but not many. The other pathway was pitch black. There was a sign that read *Off Limits to Tourists,* and it was blocked off by a red velvet rope.

"Jack," the voice said one last time. It was clear that the voice was not coming from the entrance. I quickly examined my surroundings, and as I thought, I was alone. So, I did what any normal irresponsible teenager would do. I lifted up the rope and followed the dark pathway.

I turned on the flashlight on my phone and scanned the area. For the most part, it looked extremely similar to the rest of the cave. The rock-shaped icicles dangling from the ceiling and large rocks served as walls of a building. Despite the similarities, I continued my search. I kept on walking forward attempting to spot anything out of the ordinary, and I did. There appeared to be a light blue light coming from one of the rocks. As I walked closer, I realized it was a glare coming from a rock hidden behind a smaller ordinary rock. It seemed as if someone hid it there. I moved the ordinary rock out of the way which revealed a blue crystal stone. It was flashing blue beams of light that lit up the ceiling. I admired its beauty as it appeared to have thousands of crystals embedded inside. I slowly reached out my hand and picked up the stone. It was cold as ice, so I wasn't able to hold it for more than a few seconds. This stone seemed valuable. I didn't care how much it was worth, I just wanted it as a souvenir from my senior trip. If I took the stone, it would be mine, and nobody would have one like it—almost like it was one of a kind. The cave didn't need all these rocks. They had millions, so what would be the big deal if I just took one? Well...that's what I did. I quickly grabbed the blue stone as I sprinted to try and catch up to the rest of the group.

After I caught up with the tour group, I remained at the back of the crowd. Luckily, the tour wasn't that long, so the rest of the seniors headed back to the hotel where Brian and I found Dylan dressed up in a short sleeve, white button-down, khaki pants and flip-flops with a tiny bottle of alcohol which most people referred to as a nip. He opened the bottle and chugged it in two seconds.

"Party time, boys. Get your outfits on," Dylan said excitedly. Brian and I quickly put on some nicer clothes. I wanted to look somewhat presentable on vacation. I was dressed in casual clothes, so I changed into khaki pants and a light blue, button-down shirt. I rolled up the sleeves of my shirt and quickly combed my hair. Brian came in wearing a light red polo shirt and grey khaki pants. If he had on ordinary khaki pants, he would have looked like he worked at State Farm.

"You're coming to the party, Brian?" I said surprisingly.

"Yeah, I'll stop by," he replied.

"Alright. Let's hit up this party. AYYE!" Dylan screamed as we headed down to the party.

There had to be at least 300 people packed on the beach. They had a nice set-up with a large tiki hut bar and a dance floor directly next to it.

"This is a madhouse. We are so getting in trouble," Brian claimed nervously.

"Nonsense, get a few drinks in you, and you'll be thinking very differently," Dylan said jokingly.

"Your wild party behavior is going to get all three of us in major trouble," Brian said loudly.

"Calm down. Let's just go to the bar and check it out," I said. Brian and Dylan both followed me to the tiki bar. Two blondes walked past us, and I watched one of them run her fingers down Dylan's arm. He smiled at them as they kept on walking. All three of us sat down at the bar, and the waiter quickly attended to us.

"You guys look a little young to be here," the bartender said. He was a heavy-set man with long black hair down to the middle of his back. He wore a casual white, button-down shirt with black baggy shorts. Brian stared at him nervously, and Dylan just stood there silently.

"We have IDs if you want to check," I replied.

"Take them out," he said. All three of us all pulled out our IDs. He took a quick glance at them before he nodded his head.

"Okay, what do you want?" he asked.

"We'll get two shots each of the most popular vodka you have and three martinis," Dylan said.

"I'm not taking two shots and then drinking a martini. I told you guys I was only stopping by," Brian added.

"Fine four shots total then, but still get the two martinis. You're good with that right?" he asked.

"Yeah, let's get drunk," I said excitedly. The bartender brought us over two shots each, and we drank them in a matter of seconds. Dylan and I then began drinking the martini at an accelerated speed.

"Okay, this is a recipe for disaster. I am not staying with you two guys. You're both going to be wasted in ten minutes," Brian said as he started to head back to the hotel.

"That's the point, Brian!" Dylan shouted, but Brian didn't even acknowledge his response.

"Whatever, we'll have a good time together. Brian's just missing out," Dylan said.

"Yeah. Who cares? Let's drink!" I said as we both instantly sucked down our martinis. Over the next two hours Dylan and I sat at the bar and continued our drinking spree. One martini turned into multiple beers and then another shot and another, and we were eventually absurdly drunk.

"Hhhhey, hey look...look over there," Dylan said as he pointed across the bar.

"Wwwwhat is it?" I mumbled.

"The girl dude, the girl that was giving me the eyes. I'm in dude. I'm so in. I'm going over there to put the wheels on her. Watch me," Dylan said laughing. I watched him get out of his seat and slowly stumble over to her. He was attempting to flirt with her, but it seemed like it wasn't working that well until she started to get really close to him. I couldn't believe it; all of a sudden they started making out right at the bar.

"Good for you man," I mumbled drunkenly as they began walking toward me.

"Yo, I'm gonna hang with…"

"Alicia," the girl interrupted him as it became clear that he had no clue what her name was.

"Yeah, so you'll have the room for you. Only you," he said.

"Awesome, yeah have a good night," I replied.

"Yeah, you too," he said as he stumbled away with Alicia.

I looked around, and the bar was half as empty as it was when we got there. I was so confused because I thought there were a ton of people just a minute ago. That's how I knew I was drunk. I got up and almost wiped out in the sand. I continued swaying back and forth on my walk back to the hotel focusing on trying to keep my balance. Luckily, I managed to make it back to my room alright. I ran into the bathroom, and I immediately threw up a little in the toilet. I stood and looked at myself in the mirror. I looked like a mess. My eyes were red after just puking, so I actually looked exhausted. I reached into my pocket to grab my phone but instead I grabbed the blue stone. I had forgotten I put it in the pocket of my khaki pants before we left. I examined it closely as my face got really close to it. My nose was almost touching it.

"Do you talk?" I said stupidly. "I heard something talking to me in the cave, and it wasn't my imagination. I'm Jack Colson. Who are you?" I said as I waited anxiously for a response because my drunken self thought that a stone had the ability to talk.

"Ava," a whisper said.

I heard it clear as day. I chucked the stone in the sink, shut the bathroom door, and jumped right into my bed freaking out. However, it didn't take me long to forget about what just happened and fall asleep in my bed.

My eyes opened, and I was staring directly into the ceiling light. I guess I forgot to shut the lights off. I moaned as I rolled over facing my head toward the pillow. I quickly noticed that I was sleeping on top of the blanket and still wearing the same clothes from last night. I grabbed my head as I started to realize that I had the worst headache of my life. I was aware that I drank a ton of alcohol, however, this headache was ten times worse than anything I had ever experienced. I quickly stood up, and I realized that the bathroom light was still on from the night before. I slowly walked into the bathroom as I lightly pushed the door open. I was blinded by the blue light coming from the stone in the sink. I attempted to shield the light with my hands, but it didn't work too well. After a few seconds, the light slowly dimmed enough where it was bearable to look at.

"Hello Jack," the stone said in a feminine voice. I immediately jumped back, almost banging my head on the wall. I was speechless. Motionless. Unable to comprehend what just had happened.

"I'm Ava, the Ice Queen," it said.

"Did...did you just talk?" I asked nervously.

"Yes, I am one of the four Farisphonites. You have awakened me from my ten-year rest. I was given specific instructions from the Stone Saviors to remain in hibernation so that the S.O.A.S. couldn't track my coordinates. I am one of two Farisphonites still alive, and the Farisphonites are the only beings that have the capability to destroy the S.O.A.S. However, I am not in bodily form. I require a human body with a specific bloodline to latch onto in order to unleash my true powers," she said.

"I need to sit down. My head can't comprehend all of this... and my head is killing me," I said as I grabbed the stone out of the sink and sat down on the bed.

"You are suffering from Phase One," she said.

"Phase One? I don't understand," I replied.

"The reason I was awakened was because I sensed your bloodline. It's incredibly rare. You possess an N plus bloodline. The chances that a human has that particular bloodline is one in 302.5 million. The same odds as winning the lottery. Therefore, I was able to connect with you... specifically, latch onto you. Currently you are experiencing Phase One, which is a result of the excess nykrons entering your body. They are rushing to your head quickly enabling me to attain my bodily form," she said.

"This has to be a dream." I tried closing my eyes and opening them again and again and again, but nothing changed. It was real.

"This can't be happening. I'm a high school student. I don't have N plus blood or whatever it's called. Why don't I just put you back where I found you, and we will forget this ever happened?" I said.

"You can't do that. I latched onto you for a reason. You're special. Together, we can defeat the S.O.A.S. and create a world where people decide their own fates," she replied.

"You're crazy. This is crazy. You don't have powers. I'm not special. I don't even know what is going on right now, but one thing is for sure. I'm putting you back where I found you," I said.

"No!" she screamed as a bolt of ice shot out from the stone instantly freezing the lamp on my nightstand. I stood there frozen with my eyes wide open. I hesitated to make any sudden movements. I slowly turned my head toward the door as I then proceeded to look back at the stone.

"I need to clear my head for a second," I said as I quickly exited the room breathing like I had just finished running a marathon.

Chapter Four

Austen Wolfe

I walked into my laboratory and immediately pulled out the orbuculum from my bottom desk drawer. I slowly placed it on top of the desk as I waved my hand over it.

"The event I seek is in the year 2025 when the S.O.A.S. has fulfilled its task to take over mankind," I said. I looked closely into the sphere waiting for a glimpse of the S.O.A.S.'s reign of power, but all I could see was my reflection.

"Should I reiterate myself? I requested to witness my rise to power," I repeated. I grabbed it and waited for it to show me something, but it did not. I quickly lifted it off the desk as I vigorously shook it.

"Mr. Wolfe," a voice said. I quickly turned my head to see my personal assistant standing at the door. His robotic body had just rolled into the lab. He looked like a human except for the fact that he has his two legs connected to each other. Luckily, there are wheels on his feet which allow his black metal body to move around. My eyes rolled as I slowly placed the orbuculum back onto the table.

"What is it Ottron?" I said stubbornly.

"It has come to my knowledge that the event you seek no longer exists on the current timeline. There has been an anomaly that appears to have skewed the original timeline," he said.

"How have you discerned this information? Are you certain all your parts are in their proper places?" I replied.

"I believe so sir. If you would accompany me down the hallway, I will make you aware of a particular discovery that may spark your interest, my good sir," he stated intelligently. My eyes immediately lit up.

"Let me see," I said. We left my lab and walked down a long hallway. We entered the last room on the floor. Thirty men and women were all on computers taking up almost every inch of space on each side of the room. However, a small staircase led us to the main deck where my top executives were located. There were five men and four women up there all dressed in work attire. We walked over to the central computer.

"Afternoon, Mr. Wolfe," they all said as they all nodded their heads at me.

"Ottron has informed me that you have found something that may intrigue me," I inquired.

"Yes sir," one man said. I stood next to him as he pulled up the map of the entire world. He then switched on the energy power tracker, and blue dots appeared everywhere.

"As you can see, the blue dots indicate high amounts of energy use around the United States." He clicked a few different buttons, and blue dots appeared mostly at all major companies that consume tons of energy—factories to be specific.

"This is yesterday's energy power track report," he said. He clicked a few more buttons, and the screen remained almost exactly the same, besides Bermuda. There were seven dots occupying the island of Bermuda, which was clearly odd since there were no blue dots in Bermuda on yesterday's report.

"This is today's report. Seven billion joules of energy," he said.

"Can you pinpoint a precise location, and are you sure it is not just a computer glitch?" I asked.

"I already tested it numerous times. It's no glitch. According to the report, a large amount of energy was given off at 4:43 this afternoon at the Crystal and Fantasy Caves in Bermuda. We'll keep an eye on it just in case there is another spike of energy in the next forty-eight hours. We are not entirely sure that it came from one of the two remaining Farisphonites, but-"

"It's there. Only the usage of nykrons would be able to explain the tremendous gap between the two reports. This also explains why the future whereby the S.O.A.S. creates a socialistic society in 2025 is no longer inevitable at this moment," I said interrupting him.

"Sir, it's not guaranteed that it came from one of the remaining Farisphonites. There are many other possibilities that we haven't even begun to explore," he said. I quickly pulled back my black trench coat revealing my golden revolver. I grabbed the gun as I stuck one bullet in the man's chest. He immediately dropped from his chair onto the ground. He was coughing loudly, and he likely only had another two minutes to live. He put his hand on his chest to attempt to stop the bleeding, but his efforts were useless. The other workers looked at me in silence, but I could tell they were shaking with fear.

"I am not interested in your hypothetical theories. S.O.A.S. employees that do not possess the same goal and mindset as I do are not welcome here."

"I was just trying to look at all the possibilities," the man said faintly.

"No...you are aware that nykrons are the only particles capable of harnessing that amount of energy," I said. His hand slowly fell off his chest as the rest of his body became motionless.

"Unless someone wishes to face the same fate as him, I

suggest you allow me to make the final decisions. I will send in a special force unit to extract the stone from Bermuda and ensure that it is destroyed. We can't afford to have Farisphonites compromising our goal. They will not stand in my way, and neither will any of you. I hope you realize that every single one of you are expendable...I'll be in my laboratory."

"What will you be doing sir?" Ottron asked curiously.

"Well, we need a special force unit to extract the stone, and I know just the person to lead the squad," I said smiling.

Chapter Five

LIAM SCARR

When the van came to a quick stop, we all almost flew out the windshield.

"Ready boss?" Rick asked. I nodded. Rick, Doug, and Perk picked up their AK-47s and sprinted through the large glass doors as I followed. I looked behind me and held up four fingers to Charlie so he knew how long we'd be. The place was huge with about six bank tellers behind the counter to my left.

Bang! Bang! Bang!

Typical protocol, only this time Perk accidentally shot the chandelier and glass splattered everywhere.

"Get on the ground!" Rick screamed.

"You got five seconds, or you die," Doug said. There had to be at least twenty-five people in the bank. I smiled knowing that no cop would be running in and risking twenty-five innocent lives.

"Time's up," Doug said. There was one man standing, but it didn't take long for him to drop like a dead fish. I heard Rick chuckle as the man's blood shot out, hitting a woman square in the face.

"Hey, that's not right," a man said. Rick scurried over to the man lifting him up by his collar.

"What did you say skinny?" Rick whispered to the man.

"Rick!" I screamed. He immediately looked at me as I shoved him out of the way. I grabbed the man's face as I crushed his jaw with my fist. He was motionless. He dropped to the floor in fear. I reached into my holster grabbing my black-and-white striped Desert Eagle pistol, and the man didn't stand a chance.

"Now, before you idiots waste another minute killing people, I intend to rob this bank. If you work here, stand to my left; if you don't stand to my right," I said. I watched as the frightened people quickly determined where to go.

"Men, we had only four minutes. The silent alarms have already been triggered, and the police are leaving the station now. We can't afford to waste any seconds. Rick, we don't need your lust for killing people to get in the way of the mission once again," I said. I looked down at my watch.

"Two minutes and thirty seconds left," I said. I paced back and forth as I watched tears slowly drip down a young blonde girl's cheek. I got down on a knee as I wiped the tears off her face. She looked up at me, and I smiled.

"Don't worry, it'll all be over soon," I said as I chuckled.

"Doug, lock the non-bank employees in the back room," I said as I sprung up. The five men and four women stood there in silence. I examined them closely. I attempted to read them, but they all seemed so tense due to the situation.

"I know this is a bank heist, but you all don't need to stand there like you're about to be pushed off a skyscraper," I said mockingly.

"So, which one of you knows the combination to the safe?" Perk said. I almost blew a gasket when a woman blurted out the three words that I did not want to hear.

"We don't know!"

I saw Rick's face turn bright red like a tomato. I thought his head was going to explode into a million pieces. He raised his gun and placed it on her right cheek. She jolted back immediately.

"Did that jog your memory?" Rick screamed. The woman began to sob. She tried to move away, but Rick grabbed her arm forcefully. She cried even louder as she tried to block the situation out completely.

"I don't mean to eavesdrop on your conversation, but my friend asked you a question, and it'd be rude not to answer it, don't you think?" I said as I walked closer to her.

"I don't know. I don't know. I swear," she said quickly as she was hyperventilating.

"Unless you want a death sentence, I suggest adding more words to your vocabulary," I replied.

"How about three numbers to a particular safe?" Rick added.

"I swear. I don't know," she said as she was almost having a panic attack. The other bank employees watched in horror, but they didn't budge. They remained still and refused to give us what we wanted.

"Do you want to die? Those men didn't," Rick said angrily.

"Aaaaaaah!" she screamed as she attempted to drop to the floor. She failed to reach the ground before Rick lifted her back onto her feet.

"I think you forgot to tell us something," Rick said as he loaded his gun.

"Twenty-one, eighty-seven, two," a man said quickly.

"Perk," I said.

"I'm on it, boss," he responded. I watched as he spun the knob back and forth. First twenty-one. Then eighty-seven. Last two. A total of seven seconds. Perk and Doug quickly filled the six bags with all the cash they could find. The bags were overflowing there was so much.

"And with twenty seconds to spare," I said as Doug and Perk each sprinted out the front doors with three bags each. I signaled to Rick as he had just finished locking the bank employees in the back room with the rest of the hostages... except one. The woman who blurted out we don't know. She was bawling her eyes out as she used the floor as her tissues.

"I am sorry...but it's nothing personal," I said to her quietly. I raised my pistol, and one bullet flew out instantly stopping the sobbing.

"Only three?" Rick asked. I nodded as my stopwatch hit zero minutes.

"We should get going," I told Rick. He sprinted to the car as I casually walked behind him. I turned my head for a brief second just to witness the remaining twenty-two peoples' faces pushed up against the large glass window of the back room.

"Pleasure doing business with you!" I said smiling as the bank doors swung closed.

Beep! Beep! Beep!

I reached into my pocket because my energy tracker that I had stolen from the S.O.A.S. was going off. It surprised me because it was only supposed to beep if there was an unreasonable amount of energy used somewhere around the world. I looked at the phone-shaped device, and it zoomed in on Bermuda. There were seven dots occupying the island. I wasn't too familiar with the amount of energy a single dot represented, but I knew that there was only one possible explanation for this tremendous amount of energy usage.

"One of the Farisphonites is back," I whispered to myself concerningly.

"Scarr, let's go!" Rick screamed. I quickly ran toward the van and hopped into the passenger seat. We could hear the police sirens in the distance.

"What took you so long? You're gonna get us caught," Rick said angrily.

"We have bigger problems than the cops," I said snarkily as Rick hit the gas and our van swerved onto the street.

Chapter Six

Jack Colson

I jogged toward the lobby attempting to clear my head. It wasn't working too well though. I was hyperventilating a little now, and a few families walked past me giving me dirty looks. I assumed it was because I looked like I just rolled out of bed, and I reeked of alcohol. I hadn't showered yet. I grabbed the back of my head with both my hands, so my elbows looked like they were wings. I looked around and finally decided to get water at the front desk.

"Hi, can I have some water please?" I said to the lady at the front desk.

"Sure thing," she replied as she grabbed a Poland Spring bottled water out from the mini fridge behind the front desk.

"Should I charge it to your room?" she asked.

"No, I'll pay in cash," I replied as I took out my wallet and handed her three dollars. She handed me the bottle, and I instantly began to chug it.

"Hi, can I help you?" the lady at the front desk asked. At first, I thought she was talking to me, but I quickly realized that there was a man standing next to me. He wore a white, long-sleeve, button-down shirt with not a single button undone. On top of that, he had on a dark red tie with a few white stripes. He also was wearing a tan vest which blended with his tan pants and brown loafers. His short black hair was slicked back, and he had a perfect black beard that matched it. I was still drinking the water as I moved my head slightly to gain a clearer view of the doorway. There were two black SUVs parked directly outside the hotel with two men standing next to each of them. I also noticed that the man had a Glock 22 in the holster on his right hip.

"I'm Special Agent Mark Diaz. I'm here to investigate a suspicious amount of energy usage. I need to check room 420 immediately," he said. My eyes lit up as soon as I heard room 420. I began to cough as a gulp of water went down the wrong hole.

"Uhhh, I'm going to need to ask my manager if this is okay," the lady at the front desk said nervously. He reached into his pocket and pulled out a badge.

"I'm with the FBI," he said. I was so confused. Why did they want to check my room? What's in it that the FBI is looking for? And then I remembered. The stone. They could be after the stone. Maybe they thought I took it? No matter what, I needed to hide it. My right hand began slightly twitching, and I grabbed it to attempt to control it, but it didn't work. I walked away from the front desk and as soon as I reached the staircase I began sprinting. I was jumping two stairs at a time attempting to make it to my room as fast as possible. I was freaking out, and I did not want to get in trouble.

After a minute, I reached the fourth floor, and I ran to Brian's door.

Bang! Bang! Bang! Bang! Bang! Bang!

If the noise of my fists didn't wake up Brian, I didn't know what would. Luckily, he opened the door, although he still looked half asleep in a plain white T-shirt and blue boxers. He didn't even put on his glasses.

"Jack it's not even 11 in the morning, and we don't have anything until noon," he said exhaustedly.

"Brian you gotta help me," I said as I grabbed Brian's arm and pulled him into my room. He almost wiped out, I was dragging him by his arm so fast. I closed the door behind me, and Brian used it to regain his balance.

"Ahhh, Jack I'm going back to bed," he said tiredly.

"Jack, you have returned," Ava said. I was breathing very heavily, and Brian rubbed his eyes, now more alert.

"Who just said that?" Brian said, confused. I grabbed the stone off the bed and held it up to his face.

"You need to take this stone. I took it from the Crystal and Fantasy Caves yesterday from the off-limits area-"

"You what?" he screamed concerningly.

"Look there's not much time to explain, but I was just down in the lobby and the FBI is coming up here now to check my room," I said urgently.

"No, no I can't be involved with all this. I have a scholarship to Cornell. This could ruin my scholarship if I'm seen on the news for knowing that my best friend stole an artifact from some cave," he replied.

"Brian, you need to do this. They're going to be up here any second," I said urgently.

"I can't. I can't risk it," he said as he walked out of my room. I opened the door and followed him. I grabbed his arm right before he opened the door to his room.

"Brian, I'm freaking out. You gotta help me. I swear I won't ask you for anything ever again if you do this for me," I said nervously. I heard the ding from the elevator come from down the hall.

"Brian that's gotta be them. Please," I said convincingly. He looked at me disappointed for a second before grabbing the stone and walking into his room.

"Oh, and it talks so don't be surprised if it says something," I said quickly.

"It what?" he screamed as I shut his door and sprinted back to my room.

"Okay...okay. There's nothing suspicious about my room. I didn't take anything from the Crystal and Fantasy Caves. I'm just a normal student from Brookfield Connecticut here on my senior trip," I said to myself. I looked around, and the lamp on the nightstand was still frozen solid. I quickly pushed it onto the ground, and small pieces of ice scattered around the room.

Bang! Bang! Bang!

I looked toward the door as I instantly stepped on all the ice so it would melt faster. I then slowly walked toward the door and twisted the knob with my shaking hand. I cracked the door open so they could only see my face. The man from the front desk was standing there as well as three other bulky men in black suits. They stared at me with a straight face in silence.

"How can I help you...gentleman?" I asked.

"You were just at the front desk a minute ago weren't you?" agent Diaz said.

"Yes, I was very thirsty," I replied. The men chuckled. The man from the front desk reached into his pocket and pulled out his badge.

"I'm Special Agent Diaz. We need to search your room," he said.

"Can I ask why?" I asked.

"There was an unusual amount of energy coming from your room. It was enough that it sparked the FBI's attention. That's all I can say. May we come in now?" he asked.

"Absolutely," I replied as I opened the door. The three other men quickly dispersed throughout the room. One of them was in the bathroom, one was looking through my sheets while the other one was looking through all the drawers. I was surprised that agent Diaz was the only FBI agent who wasn't searching through all my belongings. He was standing right next to me.

"What's your name?" he asked.

"Jack Colson," I replied.

"How long have you been in Bermuda?" he asked.

"This is my second day," I replied.

"Did you happen to find anything strange yesterday that you brought back to this room?" he asked.

"No, nothing strange at all. It was a pretty normal day. I'm just here on a school trip," I said as I shook my head no.

"I see. Is your hand okay?" he asked. My hand was still shaking because I was so nervous.

"It's fine...I'm not hiding anything here. I swear," I said nervously. The three other men continued searching through every inch of the hotel room before they all walked to the middle of the room.

"It's clear sir," one of the men said.

"Good. Wait in the hall for one minute."

"Will do," they said in sync as they exited the room.

"Some people think that if you say you have nothing to hide then you actually are hiding something," Diaz said. I stared at him tentatively without saying a single word. He reached into his pocket and grabbed a small business card.

"If anything out of the ordinary comes up, don't hesitate to call," he said.

"I uh, I'll let you know," I replied.

"Take care now," he said as he walked out of the hotel room and closed the door behind him.

Chapter Seven

Jack Colson

After Agent Diaz and the rest of the FBI agents left, I went into Brian's room. I opened the door, and Brian was sitting on his bed staring at Ava. It had only been a couple of minutes, so hopefully Ava wasn't getting real chatty. I don't know how Brian would react if he heard about the S.O.A.S., the nykrons, and the other nonsense that Ava was rambling on about when I first realized she could talk. Brian had put on the same clothes he was wearing last night, so he looked more presentable now. He also had on his glasses, so he looked more recognizable. Without his glasses, he looks like an entirely different person.

"What'd they say?" Brian asked.

"Oh...nothing really, just asking me a few questions, like if anything strange happened yesterday. It was no big deal," I replied.

"No big deal? The FBI just searched your room, and you're saying it's no big deal?"

"It isn't. They didn't find anything unusual, so there is

nothing to worry about. I really owe you one. Luckily, we didn't room together because you like to have your own room. I don't know how Dylan would have reacted to all of this if I had laid this whole stone stuff on him," I replied as Brian was pacing the room clearly nervous.

"This is crazy! This...this...stone talks. It claims you have some N plus bloodline that she was able to latch onto, and she needs your help to defeat some secret society called the S.O.A.S. whose goal is to attempt to create a socialist society. One where people are mindless. People will be under mind control and won't even know it. I don't know whether to believe this absurd idea, or if I'm going to wake up from a dream in the next few seconds," he said.

Now was the time when I should start to panic. Brian's incredibly smart. I mean he's going to Cornell for God's sake. This whole idea that Ava was explaining had Brian's mind going in circles. There was no way he could comprehend all of this. He has no imagination.

"Brian! Everything's going to be alright. This S.O.A.S. thing can't be real. We would know if there was a secret society controlling people from the shadows. The FBI probably came here because they think I tampered with one of the rocks in the Crystal and Fantasy Caves."

"Which, in fact, you did."

"But they have no proof. They didn't find the stone, so I'm in the clear. The main FBI agent gave me his card so I could let him know if anything out of the ordinary happens. His name is Special Agent Diaz," I said as I pulled out the business card. Ava gasped, and Brian and I both jumped.

"Special Agent Mark Diaz?" she asked.

"Yeah, what's the problem?" I replied.

"You can't trust him. Austen Wolfe has thousands of people on his payroll. Agent Diaz and a number of FBI agents are being paid off by Austen Wolfe, and they want to kill me," Ava said nervously.

"Who's Austen Wolfe?" Brian asked curiously.

"About ten years ago, a successful businessman by the name of Austen Wolfe created a secret organization called the Strings on All Society, also known as the S.O.A.S. He recruited all of the world's deadliest and richest people to work for him. Over the years, his operation has grown immensely, and they have been able to keep their organization hidden from the public. The goal is to create a society governed by them. They want to create a society where people are controlled like puppets, which means abolishing free will and the ability of people to make decisions on their own. The creation of the four Farisphonites was established around the time of the Big Bang after an alien's heart was split into four pieces. It created the red stone, the earth stone, the death stone, and me. The ice gem. Austen Wolfe has devoted the last ten years to achieving an urban legend called the Power of Four. It states that if a person or group of people are able to destroy all four stones, then that person or group will gain the powers that each stone possesses, which will enable him to use those powers to control society itself. Without a host with an N plus bloodline, my powers are useless, but with our combined strength, I can assume my powers into your body which will allow us to have a chance of destroying the S.O.A.S. for good," Ava said. I couldn't believe that there was this much at stake. I knew that these responsibilities were too great for me to take on.

"Brian, can I talk to you for a second in private?" I said as we slowly backpedaled into the bathroom. I shut the door and looked at Brian concerned.

"Do you hear all this? What is this thing talking about? It's completely insane," he whispered.

"I know but what should we do with her? She's a person. We can't just throw her out the window or something," I said.

"You need to put her back exactly where you found her," he said.

"We can't do that. She shoots ice. She has the ability to freeze objects. What if she freezes one of us? There's too much risk," I replied.

"Well, we need to put her somewhere," he said. I thought to myself for a few seconds in silence. Ava must be pretty smart, but we needed to trick her. We needed to hide her somewhere that she wouldn't expect.

"We'll hide her on the beach. There's tons of rocks there, and nobody will know the difference. I'll tell her we are meeting Dylan for breakfast on the beach, and then I'll pull her out and put her in the sand somewhere," I said.

"That's genius," he replied.

"Okay let's do it," I said as I opened the bathroom door and walked toward Brian's bed.

"We're going to meet Dylan for breakfast on the beach, and we don't want to leave you here by yourself, so we'll take you with us and then we'll help you with your mission," I said convincingly.

"Okay, that's fair," she said as I lifted her up off the bed, placed her in my pocket, and left the room.

CHAPTER EIGHT

LIAM SCARR

The waves crashed against the side of the boat as the water splashed up into the air. The boat was navy blue and white with expensive mahogany trim. Rick and I were standing in the small cabin while Charlie, Doug, Perk, and Hank all sat outside on the luxurious couches. It was a magnificent boat but not my style. Luckily, it wasn't mine. I would have never bought a boat called *Fate*.

"We're almost there, boss," Rick said. I smiled at him in silence as I opened the door to the cabin. I stared at the other men sitting on the couches toward the stern of the boat.

"Time to get your guns loaded boys," I said. The men got up immediately as they all grabbed their guns. I could see the island clearly as we quickly moved closer and closer.

We finally reached Bermuda, and Rick parked the boat on the dock directly next to the beach. The six of us quickly jumped off the boat as we examined our surroundings. I pulled out my energy tracker from my pocket, and there were still massive amounts of energy coming from this location.

"Boss, what's our plan? Are we robbing this hotel?"

Rick mumbled.

"I'll handle the hotel receptionist," Doug added.

"We're not stealing anything," I said snarkily.

"What do you mean?" Rick said angrily.

"I said we have bigger problems than the cops. We're looking for a stone. Blue or black to be specific," I replied.

"You brought us to Bermuda on what you claimed was an urgent mission to find a rock?" Perk said angrily.

"You all don't realize its significance. My old organization the S.O.A.S. is after it, and they can't get their hands on it. Not now, not never," I replied.

"No stone could be worth that much," Doug said.

"Well, it is," I replied rudely. The men looked at each other attempting to figure out what they should do. Should they listen to me or not?

"What's it gonna be? Have I ever done you men wrong before?" I said as the men stared at each other in silence. "I didn't think so," I added as I began to walk onto the beach.

The other men followed me as people began giving us dirty looks. We definitely didn't fit in. We were dressed in dark clothes as opposed to everyone else wearing swimsuits and T-shirts. I scanned my surroundings, and at first, I didn't see anything. We continued walking down the beach, and I saw it. Two kids were bending over in the sand burying the ice gem.

The one kid wore a blue, button-down shirt with khakis while the other one wore a plain white T-shirt with grey sweatpants.

"The ice gem," I whispered to myself. I examined the two kids before looking back at my men.

"That's it," I whispered.

"What's our plan?" Rick asked.

"Let's take the two kids and the stone and get the hell out of here," I replied as I quickly walked toward the two kids.

It didn't take long for me to realize that we weren't the only ones in Bermuda in search of the ice gem. There were a few very muscular men dressed in black suits starting to walk toward the two boys. They followed a shorter man who looked incredibly familiar. Special Agent Diaz of the FBI. I knew that Austen Wolfe must've instructed him to find the stone. The FBI agents reached into their jackets but not before I drew my Desert Eagle pistol and shot one of them. The hundreds of people on the beach screamed as they began to run around like lunatics. I ducked low to the ground to make myself a smaller target. The FBI agents backed up toward the hotel in order to find cover. The two kids jumped up immediately as they began to sprint away with the stone.

"Rick!" I screamed as he sprinted after them. He quickly gained ground on them and tackled them both. Bullets still filled the air, and one of them nailed Hank in the chest.

He dropped to the ground in seconds. Doug and Perk began spraying the hotel with bullets, which forced the FBI to back off.

"Hank's down!" Charlie screamed. I looked over and saw Rick had a gun at the two kids' backs. He took the stone out of the one kid's hand and quickly put it in his pocket.

Doug and Perk kept getting closer to the hotel while continuing to fire at the FBI agents. They occupied them nicely.

"The stone's freezing boss!" Rick screamed.

"I don't care about the temperature of the stone. We need to leave now!" I yelled as I sprinted toward the boat. Charlie, the two kids, and Rick all ran behind me. Doug and Perk followed, too. The FBI agents began charging closer and closer as Doug and Perk continued to run toward the boat.

BANG! BANG! BANG!

It all happened so fast. Perk dropped as Diaz stuck a bullet right on the back of Perk's head. Doug hesitated for a second before realizing he couldn't do anything.

"Let's go!" Rick screamed as Doug jumped on the boat. The FBI was getting extremely close to the dock, but by the time they reached it, we were too far out of range. We had escaped but at an expense.

Chapter Nine

Austen Wolfe

Beep! Beep! Beep!... Beep! Beep! Beep! I picked up my cell phone off my desk, surprised to see an incoming call. I wasn't expecting a phone call from anyone, and it's not particularly normal that someone would interrupt my daily business unexpectedly. I slowly held the phone up to my ear as I listened to the voice on the other end.

"Hello, Mr. Wolfe," the voice said.

"Who is speaking?" I asked clearly.

"It's Agent Diaz," he replied.

"What are the grounds for this unexpected interaction?" I asked intelligently. He paused for a second, and it was quite clear that I was going to be displeased with his response.

"We just recently discovered that a teenager named Jack Colson is in possession of the ice gem. When we first arrived, we were not able to find it in his room, but it was clear that he and his friend had it on the beach."

"Excellent. So have you formulated a strategy to capture it yet?"

"About that. It appears we aren't the only ones who are after the ice gem," Diaz replied.

"What?" I asked angrily.

"It appears Liam Scarr and a few of his companions were able to track down the stone. They kidnapped Jack Colson and his friend. We took down two of Scarr's men, but the rest of them were able to escape," he said. I stared angrily at my office attempting to formulate the next move.

"Your futile efforts to demolish one of the Farisphonites has left me with less faith in you Agent Diaz. I refuse to be bested by an insignificant gang consisting of a few ex-convicts," I said as I took a deep breath to calm myself down.

"There was nothing we could have done. We were outnumbered-"

"I am not interested in your invalid excuses...continue your search for the ice gem and report back to the S.O.A.S. headquarters in seventy-two hours. I will not take no for an answer. You will do exactly what I say even if it requires you to go against the FBI's protocol. I expect you to find the ice gem and bring Ava before me as soon as possible," I said interrupting him. He gulped as he then cleared his throat to speak.

"I will," he replied as I hung up the phone.

Chapter Ten

Jack Colson

My eyes opened, but I couldn't see anything. I looked up, down, left, and right. Nothing. I was blindfolded. I attempted to pull it off my face, but my hands were in cuffs. I was restrained. I heard some chatter coming from the car, but I couldn't make out any words. It was too difficult to listen. I was scared. I had never been kidnapped before. I had only heard stories. Kidnapping wasn't uncommon. I had seen people on the news talk about people who had been kidnapped, but I never imagined it happening to me. I knew exactly who the people who kidnapped me were, too. The Red Sinners Gang. Basically, the gang consisted of a bunch of thieves and killers led by a man named Liam Scarr. I recognized him right away. He had been all over the news for years. The criminal mastermind responsible for killing multiple people and evading the police on numerous occasions. He had short, black spiky hair with a rugged-looking blue shirt and black khaki pants. He also wore a black, short sleeve thin jacket and had a holster on his right hip, which held his legendary black-and-white striped Desert

Eagle pistol. The three other men that also made it on the boat were clearly part of the gang, too. The man that tackled Brian and I was dressed in dirty blue jeans, black boots and a plain white shirt that may as well have been brown with all the dirt on it. The man had barely any hair on his head, although he did have a 5 o'clock shadow. He also had to be at least four inches taller than I, which is really saying something since I'm around six feet tall. There was another man who was a short guy with glasses. His dirty blonde hair was parted in the middle, and it hung down like bangs. He looked like he couldn't harm a fly with his blue jeans and his *Star Wars* T-shirt. The shirt was the classic *A New Hope* movie poster. The only reason I knew that was because Brian made me watch all the *Star Wars* movies with him when we were kids. Personally, I think the movies are okay, but Brian is obsessed with them. He probably could recite quotes because he's seen the movies so many times. The last guy wore a black leather jacket with black jeans along with a plain black T-shirt underneath. He also had the black curly hair that matched perfectly with his whole outfit.

The car whipped a left turn, and I flew to the other side of the car.

"Owwwwww," Brian said quietly. I was a bit relieved that I wasn't alone in this. At least I had Brian with me.

"Brian?" I whispered.

"Yes?" he said quietly.

"You good?" I asked

"As good as I can be in a situation like this," he said.

The car made a hard right turn as Brian and I flew to the other side of the car. Brian kicked me directly in the face, and I could taste the blood coming from my lip. We came to a quick stop, and I heard the car doors open. Brian and I remained silent in the hopes that the Red Sinners gang had forgotten we were here. Unfortunately, I heard the trunk open as someone grabbed me by my leg and dragged me out of the car. I didn't try to escape though. There was no point. They had guns. I wanted to live for as long as possible. After I heard a loud thud which must have been Brian's body being thrown from the SUV, someone lifted me up by the handcuffs. I was thrown in the air and now on my feet. I felt an object pressed against my lower back. It took me a few seconds to come to the realization that there was a gun on me.

"Move it kid," someone said in a deep voice.

"I'm wearing a blindfold. I don't know where to go," I said loudly.

"Just walk straight," he said. I started to walk as he commanded. After walking for about a minute, I felt the temperature suddenly rise. There was no wind. There was heat.

"We must be in some sort of building," I thought to myself. After another minute of walking, my blindfold was finally removed along with my handcuffs. I could see again. I noticed that the huge guy was the one who had the gun to my back. I took a quick glance at my surroundings. I didn't recognize the inside of this building. It looked like a small, abandoned store. There were many shelves but nothing on them. A counter. An empty cash register. The place was stripped of everything that had any value. I jumped back as a rat ran right over my shoe. I continued forward until we reached the door.

"Open it," he said. I turned the knob as the door creaked open. We entered a small room that I'm assuming was used for storage. There was another door to the right which we walked toward. I noticed there was a sign for stairs, but it was now lying on the floor rather than hanging on the wall. As we walked through the next door, there was a narrow hallway where the lights were flickering on and off. The walls were covered with yellow paint, and someone had to just be here because the wet paint was still dripping onto the white floor. Once we reached the end of the hallway, we walked down a staircase which led us to an empty warehouse. I mean that's what it looked like. Liam Scarr and the man with the *Star Wars* T-shirt were both sitting at a large metal table.

"Stop," the huge man said quietly. We waited about thirty

seconds until the man with the black curly hair brought Brian into the room too. He stood next to me and stared at me.

"All ready Rick," the man with the curly hair said as he gave his AK-47 to Rick. He pressed the other man's gun on Brian's back now.

"Move!" he screamed in his deep voice. We both jumped as we then proceeded to enter the final room. I was almost afraid to look back because it was like looking into the eyes of a bear. It was a pretty large room, but most of the space was occupied by a large glass box. The box had two sleeping bags and a small wooden table with two chairs. Besides that, the box contained almost nothing. Only crumbs and some dried blood on the glass. The door to the box was open, so we walked toward it. When we got close enough, the AK-47 was no longer pressed up against my back. I began to turn my head toward Rick, but before I could do so I was knocked down. In the box. Only Brian and I. I stared into Rick's eyes as he locked the door to the box.

He left the room, and we were suddenly trapped. I felt like an animal. I was limited to only a confined space with only the necessities to survive. The glass box made me feel like I was dangerous. I couldn't be trusted. A recently discovered species that they couldn't comprehend. A freak of nature.

"Is that what I am?" I asked myself. Brian and I sat down

at the table in silence. There was bottled water and a slice of pizza for each of us. We sat down and ate. I pushed my hair back as I thought to myself in terror. In fear.

"What's next?" I said aloud, even though I knew there would be no response.

Chapter Eleven

LIAM SCARR

I looked around, and I could tell that Rick was trying to read me. Doug had already folded, so it was just us two. I was dealt a queen and a ten of spades. The flop and turn were already out on the table. A six of spades, a two of hearts, a king of spades, and an eight of spades. Doug flipped the next card, and it was an ace of diamonds. Rick maintained a straight face as he stared at me.

"I'll raise six," he said.

"I'm all in," I said. He looked at me in confusion. He chuckled and looked around at the other guys.

"Damn it, I'm in," he said as he pushed his chips to the middle. He flipped his cards, and he had two pairs.

"Flush," I said as I flipped my cards and smiled. Rick immediately stood up from his chair. I stared into his eyes. The eyes of a killer. The eyes of a bear right before it eats dinner.

"You think you're really funny, don't you Scarr?" he said angrily.

"Rick, just calm down," I replied.

"Taking all my money," he said.

"I'm not the one who told you to go all in with two pair," I replied.

"I'll make two pairs of bullet holes on your chest right now," he said as he grew angrier by the second.

"I'd like to see you try!" I yelled. We both reached for our guns and-

"Stop, stop, stop...it's enough!" Charlie screamed as he entered the room. Rick was breathing heavily. I could feel each breath he took like a gust of wind every few seconds. We both took a few deep breaths as we removed our hands from our guns and sat back down. I looked over at Charlie as he pushed all the cards and chips onto the floor. He dropped a pizza box on the table. He opened the box, and the blue stone was inside.

"Isn't anyone curious about what this is? I mean for God's sake, Perk and Hank just got killed attempting to steal this stone, and Scarr has told us almost nothing about its purpose besides the fact that his old organization is after it," he said.

"Seems like we need some answers," Rick said.

"I've been a part of the Red Sinners gang since the beginning. I've seen Perk and Hank kill probably more than a dozen people, and they just died because of some random mission you had us going on. I also haven't seen anyone express their condolences for our lost partners," Charlie added.

"Charlie, we know you're sentimental, but us criminals don't have hearts, so why don't you shut up," Doug said.

"It's part of the job," Rick said.

"Hold your jokes. He's got a point. I haven't told you everything about this stone," I said. Rick, Doug, and Charlie all looked at me confused.

"What do you mean boss?" Rick asked.

"What I mean is...this thing has some sort of abilities beyond our understanding. I was told a while back that during the time of the Big Bang, some alien's heart made up of unearthly technology was split into four pieces. Each piece has its own consciousness that lives inside. Without a host with a rare N plus bloodline, the stone is almost useless. However, if the stone does have a host, it has remarkable abilities. My old boss has made it his lifelong goal to destroy all four of these stones since they're the only hope for defeating the S.O.A.S.," I said.

"What's the S.O.A.S. attempting to do?" Charlie asked.

"Well, they're certainly not handing out roses. They are trying to create a socialistic society governed by them," I replied.

"We can't just sit here and let the S.O.A.S. gain control of the entire population," Charlie said nervously.

"We can, and we will. It's an inevitable future," I replied snarkily.

"It's not inevitable," a woman's voice said. Everyone jumped back in shock.

"I may have drunk a few beers, but did the stone just talk?" Rick asked.

"Yes, I can talk," it said.

"Well isn't that just incredible?" Charlie said.

"Want me to destroy it, boss?" Rick asked. I looked at the stone. The crystals were so clear, I could almost see my reflection.

"Boss?" he said again.

"No, don't destroy it. We need it. For now," I said.

"My name is Ava. I'm the Ice Queen and protector of the ice gem," Ava said.

"My, my, my, the queen has arisen. Ava, that's cute, too," I replied sarcastically.

"I would save your flirting techniques for someone else. I'm not interested in a criminal," she said. I laughed and decided to take a few steps away from the stone.

"Can someone explain what's going on?" Rick asked.

"Ava or the Ice Queen is a consciousness that is somehow inside this ice gem, which is just fascinating," Charlie said.

"Yes, that's exactly right. I'm trapped inside the ice gem so I can protect it from people destroying it," she said.

"Well I'd say you're doing a great job at protecting it," I said sarcastically.

"I'm not trying to protect it from you. I'd rather not be in the hands of a bunch of criminals, but this place is difficult to find," she said.

"Find?" Doug asked.

"I don't understand," Charlie asked.

"The S.O.A.S. is trying to find me. They need it to achieve the Power of Four," she said.

"The urban legend of the Power of Four?" Charlie asked.

"Exactly that. The leader of the S.O.A.S., Austen Wolfe, is attempting to achieve-" she began.

"Yeah, yeah we know. Look, we're not going on a little crusade to stop the S.O.A.S. We'll be dead in seconds," I said rudely interrupting her.

"That's not true. Have some faith," she replied.

"Sorry, fresh out," I replied.

"I need to assume my true form, and Jack possesses the N plus blood I need to do so. Together we can defeat the S.O.A.S."

"I'm not sure where you've developed your hopeful attitude from, but if you go up against the S.O.A.S., it'll be crushed in seconds. It's clear that we need to break the bond between you and Jack."

"You can't do that."

"Scarr, we can't break the bond," Charlie replied.

"Why don't we just kill the kids and get rid of the stupid rock?" Rick added.

"You can't kill Jack since I've already latched onto him. If he were to be killed it would be catastrophic to the universe. The energy from the ice gem would be released into the atmosphere giving thousands of people super abilities. In the wrong hands, superpowers could be extremely dangerous," Ava replied.

"And superpowers in the hands of a teenager isn't? Please," I said snarkily.

"No, not with the proper training. He's special. He can destroy the S.O.A.S. I know it," she replied.

"I'm sure you do," I replied sarcastically as I rolled my eyes.

"You could help us. We could use a skilled gunman with your knowledge of the S.O.A.S.," she replied.

"I'm not exactly in the hero business, and neither is my gang. As far as the teenagers go, I have plans for them," I said.

"Killing them," she said angrily.

"I don't want to kill them," I said laughing.

"Then what is it that you want?" she asked.

"I guess you'll find out," I said arrogantly.

CHAPTER TWELVE

JACK COLSON

This weekend, I was just living it up on my senior trip in Bermuda, and now I've been kidnapped by a bunch of criminals where I'm currently trapped in a glass box. I was fed up at this point. We had been well fed for the past two days, but we were still trapped.

"Why does he want to keep us alive?" I asked myself. It didn't make sense to me. They had barely said a word to us since they forcefully locked us up. I examined every inch of the box. There was one part that stood out in particular. The dried blood on the glass. It wasn't a ton, but it was enough to stir my thoughts.

"Whose blood is it? How did it get there? Is this person dead? Am I going to end up like that person?" I thought to myself. These questions made me light-headed, so I sat down on one of the wooden chairs. I placed my hands on my face as I thought my head was going to explode with all the questions inside it.

"Jack, are you okay man?" Brian asked. I looked up and saw him sitting across from me in the other wooden chair. His eyes were half closed, and sweat poured down his face. The whole box smelled like a combination of a football locker and a porta potty. I could not stand the stench.

"Jack," he said again. I turned my head slightly as a rainstorm of sweat erupted from my head and splattered on the table.

"I'm good," I said unenthusiastically. I lifted up my water bottle and chugged half of what was left. I took a few deep breaths as I received my second wind. I took the remaining water I had and dumped it on my head to cool me down.

"Ahhh, that's better," I said, relieved. Brian chuckled as he then proceeded to copy my actions. We both looked at each other like a couple of wet zombies and laughed. The door to the room opened. Brian and I instantly turned to see Liam Scarr standing at the entrance. It was the first time I'd ever seen him enter this room. The only member of the Red Sinners gang that came in here was Rick, and the only reason was to give us food and water. That's it. He paced back and forth a few times as he stroked his stubble beard.

"I never asked you boys your names," he said.

"I'm Brian Shadow," Brian said.

"And you?" he said as he looked into my eyes.

"Jack Colson," I said.

"Oh okay...well I'm Liam Scarr, and if you haven't heard me

say the rest of my gang members' names, I'll tell you. The big fella's name is Rick, the short guy with the *Star Wars* T-shirt is Charlie, and the other one's name is Doug. Now that we're on a first name basis, I have a few questions," he said with his snarky attitude. Brian and I looked at each other in confusion.

"Okay," I said.

"Where'd you get the stone?" he asked. "It seems like it didn't come cheap."

"I found it in the Crystal and Fantasy Caves in Bermuda," I replied. He stared at me in silence. My right hand began to shake as we looked at each other intently.

"You don't seem too special to me," he said.

"I don't care what you think of me. You're a criminal," I said confidently. His head tilted as it was clear he was surprised. He stepped closer and placed his right hand on the glass box.

"You got some mouth on you kid. I like it. What I don't like is how you used it against me," he stated as he slammed the palm of his hand on the box. He walked toward the door and opened it.

"Rick!" he shouted as he peeped his head out of the room. He held the door as Rick entered the room.

"I was just introducing myself to our little friends. This is Jack, and that's Brian," he said as he pointed to each of us. Rick nodded.

"Which one should I kill?" he asked.

"Neither. I want you to take the Brian kid into the other room. I want to talk to the mouthy one alone," Liam replied. Rick unlocked the door and signaled for Brian to come to him. Brian looked at me horrified as he slowly walked toward the door. Rick unlocked the door and put the handcuffs back on Brian. He then locked the door as he quickly guided Brian out of the room.

"Great, we're finally alone. You don't get to really know somebody unless you talk to them one on one," he said.

"What do you want with Brian?" I screamed.

"Calm down Jack. I don't have any intentions to kill you or your friend. For now," he said. I looked at him in disbelief.

"I don't trust him. He's a criminal and a liar. Why should I?" I asked myself. He maintained the same half smirk, but I still sat there in silence.

"You think I'm lying. Don't you? I wouldn't blame you kid. I know it seems like I'm as heartless as they come."

"Clearly," I said confidently. He sighed in frustration. He walked close to the glass again and placed his hand on it.

"Look kid. I've got a proposition for you. I'll let you and your friend Brian walk out of here alive if you do me one favor," he said smiling.

"Which is?" I asked.

"Your little stone friend explained that you have some N plus bloodline, and she...latched onto you. I need you and Ava to break your little bond, and then you can be on your way. We wouldn't want the S.O.A.S. chasing us like dogs."

"You know about the S.O.A.S.?" I asked, interrupting him.

"That's not important. What's important is to break this bond immediately. There's gonna be people searching for you, and if you just get rid of the stone now, you'll avoid all the trouble yet to come," he said.

"I can't do that. Ava's a person. She needs my help, and I refuse to let you boss me around. Besides, what's stopping you from killing me? Wouldn't that be an easy way to break the bond?" I said.

"I would, but I can't since that stone latched onto you in Bermuda. Killing you would release some energy into the atmosphere giving millions of people super abilities. I'd say that's not the best idea."

"You just kidnapped me. Why should I trust you?" I asked loudly.

"The only reason your friend is still alive is so you can fulfill this task. If you don't want to do it, that's fine. However, that's a death sentence. Your friend already serves no purpose to me, and he won't last the rest of the day alive. Can you trust me? Maybe or maybe not. If you want to live, then that's a gamble you're gonna need to take," he explained. I stood up from my chair and stared at Liam. He grinned, and I could tell he wanted one back.

"I'll do it!" I blurted out. His grin widened as he slowly turned around and headed toward the door. He stopped for a second and looked at me.

"Perfect," he said smiling as he exited the room.

He may have thought that everything was going to go according to plan, but I knew that I wasn't breaking the bond between Ava and I no matter what.

CHAPTER THIRTEEN

JACK COLSON

I walked into a large open room where I could see the other criminals staring at Brian and me. Ava was lying on a large metal table in the center of the room. Rick was standing behind the two of us with a gun in each of his hands. The muzzle of the gun pressed against my back. It felt like I was leaning against the tip of a knife. I was aggressively sweating through my clothes, and my hands began to shake.

"Well kid, you can say goodbye to your stone," Liam said as he slowly walked toward me. I stared at him in silence, and he looked at me with his stubble beard and half grin.

"Doug, take the stone to the location we discussed while we drop the teenagers off...wherever they please," he said.

"Yes boss," Doug replied as he quickly lifted the stone off the table and placed it in his pocket. I watched him walk toward the large warehouse doors as he walked outside.

"Let's go," Rick mumbled to us.

BANG! BANG! BANG!

We all ducked down as Liam and Charlie held up their guns. Luckily Rick removed his guns from our backs as he scanned the warehouse.

"What was that?" Charlie asked alarmed. I stood there shivering in my shoes as I heard multiple footsteps coming toward the door Doug just left out of. We all stood there silently eyeing each other. The door swung open as multiple FBI agents swarmed the warehouse. We all headed toward the door leading to the room where we were being held prisoner. Gunshots filled the room as Liam and Charlie were firing shots using the door as their cover.

"We gotta get out of here now!" I yelled.

"We got this under control!" Liam replied arrogantly.

"The stone's outside. We can't let them get their hands on it," I said concerned.

"We're all about to get a few extra holes in us, and you're talking about the stone now?" Liam screamed.

"She needs our help!" I thundered.

"Jack, we can't help her," Brian whispered.

"What are you gonna do about it anyway? There aren't many exits if you haven't realized," Liam said. I suddenly remembered there was an exit directly to the right of this door. I poked my head out for a second just to see how close the FBI agents were. They were close, but I had some room. I took a deep breath as I pushed Liam and Charlie out of the way and immediately bolted to the exit.

"Jack!" Brian screamed after me.

"What the hell are you doing?" Liam bellowed.

I didn't stick around long enough to respond. I was in a full sprint to the door as bullets flew around me. I bulldozed the door as I successfully made it outside. I quickly noticed that Doug was lying on the pavement outside the warehouse door. I ran over to him and grabbed Ava out of his pocket. Two FBI agents came flying through the other door and started shooting at me. I ran toward the woods across the street as fast as I could, but they were gaining on me. Bullets were bouncing off trees and branches all around me. I tried to ignore it, but it was difficult. I mean I was being shot at by two FBI agents.

Bang! Bang! Bang! Bang! Bang!

There was no cover around me, and the bullets seemed to be getting closer to hitting me. I was taking long deep breaths. I stopped and kneeled down behind a tree.

"Jack," I heard Ava say from my pocket.

"What?" I replied.

"Use me as a weapon," she said. I lifted Ava out of my pocket as I firmly gripped her. I reached my hand out from the tree. Bullets started to fly, but Ava released two blue light beams that halted the gunfire. I cautiously swung my head around the side of the tree and saw the two agents were frozen solid. I sighed in relief as I rested my back against the tree and sat down.

"Jack, your shoulder!" Ava screamed. I looked at her confused. I slowly twisted my head and noticed that my shoulder was bleeding. I had been shot. Luckily, the bullet had just grazed me, so nothing had to be surgically removed. If Ava didn't tell me that my shoulder was bleeding, I wouldn't have even known. My adrenalin was so high I didn't feel it. However, I almost started to panic looking at it, but I decided to remain calm.

"What do I do? Where should we go?" I asked Ava nervously.

"What time is it?" she asked.

"I said where should we go not-"

"Just what time is it?" she said, interrupting me.

"It's 10:15," I stated.

"Okay, keep walking straight, and we'll find him," she said.

"Find who? I asked stubbornly.

"An old friend who can help me and you. Now, let's start moving," she said eagerly.

"What about my shoulder?" I shouted. A light blue beam slowly shot out of her as it landed directly on the wound. My shoulder was an icicle. I screamed until I was out of breath. I placed my hand on my shoulder, and I felt its rough texture. I was wearing a shirt which slightly protected my body from the cold ice that stuck to my body. I sat there hyperventilating for a minute, and then the ice suddenly vanished.

"What just happened?" I asked.

"It's called quick freeze. The cold only lasts for a minute. Once that time hits, the ice instantly melts and vanishes within seconds," she said.

"Wow," I said in amazement.

"That should slow the bleeding down for now, but we need to start moving," she said. I slowly stood up and we began our journey.

Chapter Fourteen

Liam Scarr

Bullets flew back and forth ricocheting off the walls. Jack had just risked his life to go after the stone, and now Rick, Charlie, Brian, and I were cornered. Rick fired a shot that took down one of the FBI agents, but there were still at least five of them closing in on us.

"Boss, we got to do something quick," Charlie said urgently.

"I know," I said looking around the room. There appeared to be no way out. Besides the glass box, the room was mostly empty. I examined the concrete walls hoping to find an exit, but there wasn't one.

"Push up! Push up!" I heard Agent Diaz scream from the other room.

"Boss!" Rick screamed as he continued firing shots. I moved closer to the door and fired three shots at the fuse box, and the warehouse went black. Rick unloaded shots into the darkness, and I heard some screams.

"Fall back! Fall back!" Agent Diaz shouted. I couldn't see anything, but I knew exactly where to go.

"Charlie, grab the kid," I said as I sprinted toward the exit while Rick, Charlie, and Brian followed. We ran up the stairs to the long hallway with the wet paint dripping down the wall. It was brighter in this room, which made it clear that the FBI agents definitely weren't far behind. Charlie and Brian just made it up the stairs before one of the agents fired at the staircase.

"They went up the stairs!" he bellowed. The four of us sprinted down the hallway without turning our backs for a second. I bulldozed through the last door leading us to the main entrance of the abandoned store. Rick and I were quickly met by two agents who tackled us to the ground making us drop out guns. I quickly knocked the man's weapon out of his hand and punched him in the face.

"Get to the van!" I screamed to Charlie as he ran out the main entrance holding a gun to Brian's back. The other man was giving Rick a run for his money. He hit Rick in the face, but then Rick stood up and threw him to the ground. It didn't take long for Rick to start hitting him profusely with no intention of stopping. I stood up and attempted to reach for my gun, but the man threw me up against the wall and punched me directly in the stomach. I hunched forward trying to deal with the pain, but once he hit me again, I fell to the ground. I looked over at Rick and signaled for him to watch the hallway. He stood up, grabbed his assault rifle, and began firing shots down the hallway. I then proceeded to jump on the man's back, which stopped him from grabbing his gun. The man hit his head hard on the ground, and he laid there for a second or two. I quickly ran over to my pistol, snatching it off the floor but not before the man grabbed my waist attempting to throw me to the floor once again. I aggressively pushed the man off of me as my arm did a 180-degree turn. My pistol whipped him in the side of the head, and he dropped instantly. I looked outside to see that Charlie had pulled our blue van directly in front of the main entrance.

"Rick!" I screamed. He turned around, and I motioned for him to follow me to the van. The two of us thrusted ourselves into the back seat as Diaz and two other agents opened the door to the abandoned store just in time to see our van pulling out of the parking lot.

Chapter Fifteen

Jack Colson

The wind punched my cheeks. I was cold, scared, and useless. The mud was controlling me, almost eating me up like its prey. I slowly walked forward as the vines ripped away at my khaki pants. I was still in disbelief that I escaped the FBI. However, my shoulder was still bleeding. It made me nauseous just looking at it. I looked up, and I was able to see a bald eagle flying above me. I smiled.

"Hey over here...hey!" a man called out in the distance. I looked over to see an old man walking his dog and waving his hands in the air.

"Hey over here...!" he yelled again.

The man pointed behind him and whispered something to his dog. He then slowly approached me as his dog immediately sprinted the opposite way. He wore a blue jay, plaid flannel shirt with baggy blue jeans. On his hands, he wore dark gray fingerless construction gloves. The color of his gloves matched his gray work boots that looked like he'd been wearing since he was 12. They were filled with scratches and a few holes on the sides. As he walked closer, I noticed his large gut pressed up against his shirt. It looked like there was a bowling ball under his shirt. He had his three top buttons undone along with his bottom button. There were only three buttons stopping his stomach from being exposed. His gray chest hairs hung freely as they slowly swayed through the wind. His hair was thin, but it covered his head enough where he wouldn't be classified as bald.

"This is him," I heard Ava whisper from my pocket.

"Who? The friend?" I asked as I removed Ava from my pocket.

"Looks like you found yourself quite the gem I'd say," the old man said in his soft voice.

"Yes, it's beautiful," I replied.

"Did she tell you to come here?" he said pointing to Ava.

"Yeah, she said you're a friend, and we can use your help," I told him. He stared at me and signaled for me to follow.

"Come with me. I have a more private place where we can talk," he said.

After following the man for a few minutes, we arrived at a small log cabin. The house was surrounded by thousands of trees that stood as tall as the redwood trees in Muir Woods. There were no other houses around us, and the only sounds that I heard came from the crows that flew above us. I don't think there was a street within miles; it was us and the woods. We entered the cabin, and his blonde labradoodle immediately jumped on me. It was huge. I fell back and almost wiped out when the thing pounced on me. On its hind legs it was taller than me. I squatted down as I began to slowly pet his head. His hair was soft. It grabbed my fingers as I stroked my hand through.

"His name's Cooper," the old man said with a smirk.

"Oh, what a nice name," I said as Cooper's tongue touched every inch of my face. His saliva shot out everywhere and covered my face. I used my shirt to wipe it off as I stood up. Even after I stood up, Cooper's face was slobbered with saliva as he began to drool all over the floor.

"Come, let's talk," he said.

His cabin was cozy. His couch looked soft, and his rug was made out of some type of animal fur. It was clear this man was some sort of a hunter because there were items made out of animal fur everywhere. A deer's head also hung from his wall. I followed the old man down a hallway until we reached a sliding glass door.

"After you," he said kindly.

"Thanks," I said as I walked onto his back porch. It was small but nice. There was a white wooden Adirondack chair, a brown wooden rocking chair with a cushion on it, and a small brown table between them.

"Please, sit," he said as he pointed to the white Adirondack chair. I watched as he grabbed a Mountain Dew can from a cooler on the deck.

"You thirsty?" he asked.

"No, I'm fine, thanks," I replied.

"Suit yourself...so let me see the ice gem," he said. I took Ava out of my pocket and placed her on the table.

"It's been a long time since I've seen you last," he said to Ava.

"I know, but I'm desperate for your help. The S.O.A.S. has found me. They tracked me to Bermuda after I called out to Jack. He possesses the unique N plus bloodline. I latched onto him, and he is our only hope for stopping the S.O.A.S.," she said. He looked at her shocked.

"Impossible, nobody has had an N plus blood type in years. All those years ago I brought you to Bermuda so you could go into hibernation and now...now you've found a way. A chance to stop the S.O.A.S.," he replied.

"I know, but I...I...I used my abilities," she said nervously. The old man sighed.

"Why? Why did you use your powers?" he asked.

"To show Jack. He originally refused to help me. He didn't believe me," she said. He looked up at me with a calm expression.

"So rude of me, I never introduced myself. My name is Paul

Jankins. And you are Jack?" he asked.

"Colson, Jack Colson, nice to meet you," I responded as I shook his hand. His hand was extremely smooth. He grasped my hand, and it was like touching a marble counter. He had a unique presence. A calming presence. It was weird, but I enjoyed it.

"So, Ava called out to you," he asked me.

"Yes, she was calling my name like a whisper in the Crystal and Fantasy Caves in Bermuda," I said.

"It may seem scary now, but trust me, she means well. She's got a good heart," he replied as I smiled.

"Okay, but we actually have a problem. What am I going to do about the S.O.A.S.?" she asked concerned.

"Well first, start by not using your powers at all. The more you use them, the easier it will be for them to find you. Number two, you should hang here for a while. It's safe. There's nobody within miles of here. And lastly, calm down. Everything will be just fine," he said calmly.

"Wait, hold on. I'm a little confused. How do you know Ava, and how do you know so much about the S.O.A.S.?" I asked. He sighed.

"Let me take it back to November 11, 2001. Nineteen years ago. At that time, they called me Lieutenant General Jankins of the U.S. army. I was second in command behind General

Wolfe. Austen Wolfe. I was in my late forties at the time, and Austen was only in his mid-twenties. He may have been the general, but I was like a father to him. We were extremely close. I taught him everything he knows. He was an extremely skilled soldier, and on top of that, he was a genius. He was gifted with knowledge and fighting—the smartest man I knew. We were on a small voyage in Iceland, and there were reports of a planned attack group in the country. According to the reports, they were planning to assassinate President George W. Bush because they were infuriated about the 2000 election. Luckily, it was just rumors. There was no attack group in Iceland. The whole voyage was for nothing. However, the best fifteen soldiers were sent to Iceland on a submarine called the *Blue Marlin*. On the coast of Iceland, our unit came across a gem—the ice gem to be specific. A blue light was blinking every four seconds at the bottom of the ocean. Austen and I, being the two highest ranked soldiers, put on scuba diving gear and retrieved the unknown object. It didn't take long for Ava to reveal herself as the Ice Queen and the Farisphonite who has vowed to protect the ice gem at all costs. The other soldiers believed that we should bring it back to the U.S. and deliver it to the president, but Austen... he didn't think so. He thought we should keep it for ourselves, and once he realized Ava's true abilities, he became...obsessed.

He was consumed by this mystical urban legend called the Power of Four. The legend stated that if a person were to destroy all four of the stones, then they would be able to obtain a power beyond our understanding. One that enables a person to have unlimited power over people and the decisions made amongst the world.

"On our journey back to the States, Austen started to change. His true self was put behind him, and a self-centered egomaniac was formed. One unlike the Austen Wolfe that I used to know. Once we reached the States, the soldiers attempted to take the stone from Wolfe because they knew that he shouldn't keep it. It wasn't right. Unfortunately, he killed them all. Slaughtered them. I was dismayed that he went to such extreme lengths to keep the ice gem in his possession. I was horrified by the man he had become, and once I discovered his numerous books pertaining to the Power of Four, I immediately took action.

"It was about two weeks after the discovery when I snuck into his room late at night and stole the stone. I attempted to be quiet, but I failed. He woke up and instantly screamed at me. I told him it was for his own good, but he didn't believe me. He started to throw punches at me, and I was forced to fight back. After I finally got the upper hand on him, I pulled out my gun and I shot him in the thigh. He screamed in pain.

I was deeply upset and agitated as he laid on the floor. He was hopeless, but his eyes lit up like fire. It was an anger I've never seen before. I had the chance to end it all. To kill Austen Wolfe, but I couldn't. I just couldn't do it. I was torn as to what to do, but in the end I just left him there.

"I took the gem to Bermuda, and I hid it in the Crystal and Fantasy Caves. I told Ava where I would be if she ever needed my help. It's nineteen years later, and somehow, she has ended up in your hands," he told me.

I didn't know what to say. It was a lot to take in.

"I trust you," I said as he smiled back at me.

"That's good to hear. Now why don't you both go inside and get some rest," he said as we stood up and walked back in the cabin.

 AVA

Thousands of people crowded around each other. There were no seats to watch the press conference, so the people were forced to stand. The cameramen were ready, and the news reporters had their microphones on counting the seconds until the clock struck four. The sun had almost set, and the temperature was below freezing, so people had their winter jackets and gloves on. I sat on the stand on center stage. I was there, but I wasn't the center of attention. The crowd was cheering so loudly but once 4 o'clock hit, you could hear a pin drop. President Corban Rugs walked onto the stage and smiled down at me. He wore a black suit with a yellow tie. His hair was blonde, and it covered his entire forehead. He waved to the people, and they all cheered. The people loved Corban. He was a humble, honest man and he cared for all the people of Iceland. He was like the father I never had.

"Attention people of Iceland. I'm so glad that you were all able to join me on this amazing day," he said. The crowd cheered so loudly, they probably heard us in the States.

"Today, I'm proud to announce that the war with the

Germans has ended. We were able to agree upon a peace treaty. The treaty has enabled Iceland to be free of German rule. As of today, February 29, 1916, Iceland is now its own independent state. I am proud to call this my home!" he exclaimed. He held me up in the air, and the crowd went wild. The people of Iceland were extremely happy to finally gain their independence from the Germans.

"You did it. You freed Iceland from German rule. You are a real hero," I told Corban.

"I shouldn't take all the credit. You helped, too," he replied smiling. I heard a faint noise in the distance. It sounded like a plane. We looked in the distance, and we saw ten planes heading towards us. The people were still jumping up and down with joy. They didn't even acknowledge the planes. Corban looked down like it was nothing. He believed they were just passing by, but I thought it could be some sort of attack. I wanted to say something—anything to alert Corban of what I thought was yet to come. But I didn't. I didn't say anything.

The planes flew over us, and people quickly went from happy to scared. Heavy gunfire filled the press conference, and it was all my fault. I knew what they wanted. They wanted me. They wanted to use me as their military weapon.

I was able to freeze one of the planes, and it immediately

lost all control, shattering like glass once it hit the ground. Corban picked me up and quickly ran to shelter. Hundreds of people laid motionless on the ground. It was tragic, and I felt responsible. The military planes continued to fly over us and shot at any living creature they saw. The people screamed in both pain and fear. I wanted to cry. I was clueless as to what the people should do. The firepower was too strong for the buildings to endure, so people kept running in and out of the buildings hoping not to get wiped out. I began to cry as water slowly dripped out of the ice gem into Corban's hand.

"Ava, we'll be alright," Corban said. I didn't say anything. I just continued to sob. After a few minutes, the bullets from above stopped. The planes landed in the center of town, and German troops quickly left the planes and scattered all over the town. The screams got worse as more people were shot down. People were dropping like flies. Corban ran out of the building in an attempt to reach the shoreline. Two agents fired shots at us, but I immediately turned them into ice sculptures. It was too difficult to watch. I wanted to scream after seeing thousands of people being shot down in a matter of minutes. Corban continued to run. He sprinted as far as possible. Fortunately, the press conference was held close to the shoreline. He ran and ran until he reached the southern tip of the coast; however, we were a thousand feet above sea level. There was nowhere to go. Nowhere to hide. It didn't take long for more soldiers to quickly converge on our location. I froze a few of them, but there were just too many. I focused as I created a forcefield around us.

"Ava," Corban whispered to me.

"What?" I replied.

"You can't protect me anymore. We both can't make it out of this alive," he said.

"No, we can. We can," I told him.

"No. We can't. You can't hold that forcefield up much longer. You can escape. They're after you. I'll help you," he said.

I started to get teary eyed. I knew exactly what he was saying, knowing it was true. We both couldn't make it out alive or without getting captured. I froze away my tears and realized what had to happen.

"Okay. Help me," I said.

"I will. Just trust me," he said smiling. I looked at him, and he looked back at me. I could tell he was holding back tears, but so was I. The men continued shooting, and they began to get extremely close. The men were within fifteen feet, and I couldn't hold the forcefield for much longer.

"Goodbye Ava," he said smiling.

"Goodbye Corban," I replied, barely able to get my words

out. He pulled his arm back and released me into midair. The forcefield disappeared as I left his hand, and I watched as the German soldiers unloaded all of their bullets into Corban's back. He dropped in a matter of seconds, and we both fell into the ocean.

I hit the water and began to cry my eyes out. I sunk to the seafloor alone. By myself. No one left in my life. I was afraid for my future. I wondered if I would remain down here for all eternity. I asked myself if anyone would ever find me down here, and if someone did, would they be half the person Corban Rugs was. I screamed at the top of my lungs in fear, but the only person to hear it was me.

Chapter Seventeen

Austen Wolfe

I sat impatiently at my desk awaiting the FBI unit's return. They were scheduled to report back to my office upon their arrival. They had given me no updates on the ice gem, and all they'd told me was that they would meet me in my office at 5:00. It was 6:30, and I was done waiting.

"Ottron!" I screamed.

"Yes sir. How can I assist you?" he replied as he slowly walked into the room.

"Any word from the FBI unit?" I asked.

"Yes, I have just gotten word that they have arrived," Ottron said.

"Perfect, send them in," I said as I gave him a fake smile.

"Will do," he replied.

"Oh, and make sure you have one of the maids replace your battery. It hasn't been changed in a week. Your battery is definitely low," I told him.

"I will certainly do that," he replied as he slowly left the room.

I looked up and was astonished that there were only three

people standing in front of me. I quickly jumped from my chair and looked outside my door. There was no one else standing out there. I slowly walked back to my chair and placed my feet on my desk. I grabbed my glass of water and chugged the rest of what was left. I started to take long, deep breaths. It's a method I use to calm myself down. I grabbed the collar of my shirt and lifted it up. I loosened my tie and tossed it on the side of my desk. I then unbuttoned the top button of my shirt.

"Thank God. I'm not being choked by that damn tie anymore," I said as the two agents chuckled.

"So, is this it? I send you out there with nine men, and you come back with two. What happened?" I said loudly.

"The teenager Jack Colson and his friend were there accompanied by Liam Scarr and a few of his skilled thieves," Agent Diaz said.

"And the ice gem...where is it?" I replied angrily.

"Jack Colson escaped with it into the woods," he said.

I flipped through papers until I found one that was labeled geographical maps. I spread one of the maps across my desk. Agent Diaz intensely examined the map and placed his finger on it.

"There. That's it," he said.

"It seems like the gem must be somewhere in these woods

behind the warehouse. Unfortunately, it's too much ground to cover, especially with the limited agents I have available. The ice gem is also dangerous, and I don't want to risk losing a hundred men because they go into an unknown area. We don't know who we are up against. I don't know who these teenagers are or these other men, but we need to find out fast," I said eagerly.

"We need to find someone who knows the area," he said.

"That's it. I know this woman named Violet who served as a green beret in the Army Special Forces. She's an expert in jungle warfare and has extensive knowledge in geographical terrain. If we get her help, it would be a substantial advantage in locating the whereabouts of Jack Colson and the ice gem."

I pulled out my phone and began dialing numbers. The phone started to ring for a few seconds until it came to halt. I heard breathing on the other end, so I knew she was there.

"Violet, I have an assignment for you."

Chapter Eighteen

Special Agent Diaz

Chatter filled the air as FBI agents surrounded the home of the closest connection to Jack Colson and Brian Shadow. I walked up to the door and gave it three hard knocks. After a few seconds, I was greeted by a young, six-foot-tall, athletic-looking man with long blonde wavy hair. He was slovenly dressed wearing blue jeans and a Brookfield High School T-shirt.

"Are you Dylan Kennedy?" I asked.

"Umm, yes," he replied.

"I have a few questions regarding your friends Jack Colson and Brian Shadow," I stated.

"Alright," he said, nodding.

"Tell me everything that you remember about your trip to Bermuda before your friends disappeared, and try to be as specific as humanly possible," I asked.

"Well, the three of us arrived in Bermuda around midday. Brian was going on one of his nerdy tangents about how we need to follow the school's agenda and visit the Crystal and Fantasy Caves. I told him that he needed to relax and let loose a bit. Obviously, he didn't. Brian and Jack decided to go to the Crystal and Fantasy Caves when I just kicked back in the room and watched some television. By the time they came back, I told them that we were going to this awesome tiki party on the beach. Brian didn't stay that long because he was afraid of getting in trouble, but Jack and I were doing some drinking. It was a ton of fun. I even met this girl there who I ended up going home with and…and," he said enthusiastically before stuttering his few words.

"And?" I asked.

"And…they were gone. I haven't seen them since," he said sadly.

"Did you happen to see anything strange in your room? Anything at all?"

"No, there was nothing out of the ordinary."

"Okay…I guess that'll be all then."

"I'm sorry. I know I haven't been much help."

"It's okay. I hope you feel better," I said as I patted him on the shoulder.

"Thanks," he replied as he shut the door. I sat down on the concrete and sighed in frustration. I sat there in silence as I played with a few pebbles on the road. I was tossing a few rocks back and forth in my hands. It was like a game of hot potato that I never wanted to end. I wanted to do anything that would distract me from life itself.

CHAPTER NINETEEN

AVA

The lights flickered on and off like a strobe light. The escalators were turned off by this point. I could hear many people screaming from outside Caesars Palace. The place was basically empty. There was some blood from the agents scattered around the casino. Four FBI agents laid on the carpet floor motionless. There were two agents walking around near them. I guess they were checking if they were still alive. They weren't. There was no chance. The floor was covered in empty shells and bullets. The casino looked like a war zone. The playing cards still sat on the poker tables as if a game was still going on. There were also tons of chips still on the table, too. It looked like everyone was having a pretty lucky night. There were loud footsteps coming from the floor above. It sounded like someone was running a forty-yard dash. The sound of the footsteps increased as Liam Scarr jumped onto the escalator and slid down the railing. He had his gun ready and instantly fired two shots at one of the agents. The one agent dropped to the floor while the other continued to fire. Rick slowly jogged behind Liam, and they both took cover behind one of the poker tables.

"I got him, boss," Rick said as the last agent fell.

"Nice. You stay here. I got this covered," Liam said arrogantly.

"We're partners, aren't we? You think you're some kind of hero, but you're nothing more than a self-centered thief," Rick stated.

"Yeah, well you're nothing more than a bear. You got the muscle but not the brains," Liam responded as they both quickly stood up.

"You're going to risk your life for some kid!" Rick shouted.

"Yeah," Liam said quietly. He slowly pulled out his pistol and struck Rick in the face with the gun. Rick went out like a light and slowly collapsed.

"I am sorry Rick...but only one man is risking his life today...and it's me," Liam said quietly as he slowly proceeded through the casino.

Beep! Beep! Beep!

"Rise and shine," I heard Paul say from another room. Jack got out of bed, and he finally looked like he had gotten some good sleep for once. He picked me up and carried me into the kitchen where Paul was making breakfast.

"How was the sleep?" Paul asked.

"Great, yeah it was really good," Jack responded.

"Not that good. I, uh...I had a vision," I said.

"A what?" Jack asked.

"A vision," I repeated.

"What do you mean?" Jack asked. Paul chuckled as he stared at Jack.

"You don't know much about the ice gem do you, boy?" he asked.

"No, I mean I know she can freeze objects...and people," Jack said.

"Ava can do much more than just freeze objects and human beings. She possesses abilities that are out of this world. She is one of the two Farisphonites that are still alive. The King of Fire, Max, was killed by Austen Wolfe a few years back along with the Earth God, Shane. All that remains is Ava the Ice Queen and Miya the Death Goddess," Paul replied.

"Where is this Death Goddess Miya now? And how did Austen Wolfe manage to kill two of the Farisphonites? And-"

"Take it easy. I can't answer a hundred questions all at once. The whereabouts of the Death Goddess are unknown. Nobody has seen her in years. As far as how Austen Wolfe managed to kill two of the Farisphonites, those are stories for another time. I'm also curious like you Jack. I want to know about Ava's vision. One of her abilities is that she is able to have visions of the future. The future is constantly in flux, so nothing is set in stone. It's always in motion. It's always changing, so it is hard for her to determine if the vision will definitely occur," he said, cutting Jack off.

"Yeah, I had a vision of Caesars Palace in Las Vegas. I don't know if I was there or you were there. However, Liam Scarr and Rick were definitely there along with some of Wolfe's agents. They were briefly discussing whether or not to go back for some kid. I shouldn't go into the specifics because it isn't good for ordinary people to know too much information about the future. I will tell you that I'm scared. I think your friend Brian or you may be in some unexpected danger. Same with the remaining members of the Red Sinners gang," I said nervously.

"And you," Jack asked.

"Most likely," I replied.

"Well, what am I supposed to do? Just sit here? I care about Brian. I don't care about the Red Sinners gang. They kidnapped me for God's sake. But...if they care enough to go back for Brian or me, then I guess I do care about their fates," Jack replied.

"Relax, relax...Ava's vision shouldn't influence your next actions. You should remain here like your original plan. The more you change your thought process, the more the future will change for the better...or for worse," Paul replied.

Chapter Twenty

LIAM SCARR

"Well isn't this just great?" Rick bellowed in his deep voice. A few droplets of saliva slid off his lip into the air. His gruff scream was followed by a thud. The garbage can now lay horizontally on the floor. The beer bottles, wasted food, and candy wrappers poured out onto the floor of the worn-down down apartment we just bought.

"Cool it, Rick," I said.

"Well, the kid is gone. We spent all night looking for him and found nothing. Our hideout was raided by the FBI, and now we're staying in some hell hole of an apartment in Brookfield," he replied.

"Tell me something I don't know," I stated. He stared at me angrily as he grunted like a hungry animal.

"Liam, what are we going to do about Jack? We need to find him," Brian asked.

"Well, we have no clue where Ava and Jack would want to go," I responded.

"Probably someplace Ava feels safe because Jack has never been in those woods before," Brian said. I looked at him, and my eyes opened completely wide. A light bulb went off in my head.

"Wait, that's it! Someplace where SHE feels safe. Charlie!" I shouted.

"Yeah?" he responded from another room.

"Fire up the Blue Mystique. We are taking a ride to Knuckleheads," I said loudly.

"What's the Blue Mystique?" Brian asked. I smiled and signaled for him to follow me. We walked outside the apartment and pointed to the van in the parking lot. The Red Sinner's signature van. It was blue with black stripes. The car looked like it was bought today. There were no dents or holes. The tires were shining, and the mirrors had no smudges.

"You named the van?" Brian asked.

"Yep, this baby has gotten us out of some tough situations. It's our most prized possession," I said. Brian slowly walked forward. He examined the car from front to back.

"Are we ready?" Charlie asked as he came out from behind the car.

"Yeah...Rick, let's move," I said. Rick jogged outside of the apartment, and we all jumped in the car. Rick turned the key, and the engine roared like a lion.

"There we go," Rick said as he chuckled. He then quickly switched gears, and we were off.

We pulled up in front of the bar. The sign read Knuckleheads Saloon. It was a dive bar. We walked in, and it was the classic bar scene. There were pool tables, a dartboard, tons of drinks, and a bartender who'd worked here for about fifty years. A few people started to whisper to one another once we walked in. The place was crawling with bikers, rednecks, and criminals. One big fella with an eye patch gave Brian a look. I saw him immediately look away and try to pretend that the man was just a figment of his imagination. They had the band Thunderstorm playing tonight, which was no surprise because they played here almost every night. Their country music was soothing, and it fit the calm mood of the bar.

"Hey Liam, how are you doing man?" Ron shouted across the bar.

"Pretty good," I responded.

"You're here to celebrate that bank heist the other day?" Ron asked.

"No, actually we are here on more of a business matter. I'm looking for Wayne. Is he here?" I asked.

"Yeah, he's in the back," he responded.

"Perfect," I said.

"Yo Liam, who's the kid?" Ron asked.

"He's with me. He's uh...a new member of mine," I replied.

"Oh, do the boys want the usual?" Ron asked.

"Yeah, just bring mine to the back," I said.

"Sounds good," he replied. I started to walk to the back room. I watched as Ron greeted the rest of the guys and introduced himself to Brian.

"You guys stay here," I told Brian, Charlie, and Rick.

I then proceeded to open a door into the back room of the bar. There was a small couch with a ton of rips in the cushions. The room had brick walls and a dark red rug in the middle to match them. Wayne was seated on the couch with two strippers. He wore grey sweatpants, a baggy T-shirt, and his hair was a mess. He wasn't even wearing shoes. He was barefoot, and the strippers were dressed in bikinis that were two sizes too small. A 16-year-old girl could have pulled off that outfit. They rubbed their hands against him like they were bathing him. He was smiling as things were about to speed up, until he realized I was in the room.

"Hi there," I said mumbling.

"Oh, hey Scarr. What are you doing?" he said.

"Can we talk...in private?" I said rudely.

"Oh, yeah yeah, sure man...ladies give us a minute," he said as the strippers left the room, rolling their eyes at me. They were clearly irritated that I interrupted their little hangout.

"I was wondering if you've ever heard of the ice gem?" I asked Wayne.

"Yes, I've heard of it. The urban legend of the Power of Four," he said.

"I thought you'd be the man to know about it. You're into a lot of that fantasy type stuff," I said laughing.

"Yeah, I love it. The Power of Four is actually a truly fascinating legend. Sometimes I'd imagine what the world would be like if the legend was actually true," he said excitedly.

I rubbed my eyes. I wasn't sure if I wanted to go through with asking him about the gem. I like Wayne. He knows his stuff about urban legends and all that mystical crap, but the man's an idiot.

"Look, I have a few questions about the ice gem. I want to know if-"

"What's this about?" he said, interrupting me. I looked at him and attempted to create a believable excuse.

"I'm, uh...writing...writing a paper about...the Power of Four," I said.

"Oh okay. Well, what would you like to know?" he asked.

"Okay, hypothetically let's say that this whole Power of Four legend is real, and someone is actually attempting to achieve it. Who...who are the...the heroes of the story?" I asked.

He looked pensive. It took about a minute for him to respond.

"Well, in the story there was a small group of people that

called themselves the Stone Saviors. They were a group of people who vowed to protect the four Farisphonites from anyone who attempted to achieve the Power of Four. They were able to help the Farisphonites from being killed in the story. They would be considered the heroes alongside the four Farisphonites," he stated.

"Where were these Stone Saviors-"

"What are you looking at kid?" someone screamed from the other room.

"Nothing, I, uh, uh..." I heard Brian say from the other room.

"Yo Liam, your friends are in a bit of a predicament," Ron said as he swung the door open. Wayne and I sprinted out the door, and the guy with the eye patch was right up in Brian's face. Brian was shaking in terror. This man had to be three hundred pounds of pure fat. He was six foot two though, and he looked like he could eat Brian for dinner.

"Sir, this is a complete misunderstanding. My friend here-"

"Your friend should watch himself," he said, cutting Charlie off.

"Hey, if there's a problem. You take that outside," Ron yelled.

"Well, I have a problem with the kid!" the eye patched man yelled back.

"Look, I don't want any trouble. I...I didn't mean to upset you," Brian said nervously.

"Upset me?" the man said.

"You want to keep that other eye?" Rick mumbled as he held a knife to the guy's head. Now the room was filled with screams, and in a fit of rage, Rick cleaned the guy's clock real fast. The floor shook as the eye patched man fell to the floor. A few men who were sitting behind him stood up and immediately went after Rick. Tables flipped, glass cups shattered, and punches were flying everywhere. Charlie and Brian immediately took cover behind the bar. They wanted no part of the fight. Ron and I intervened and attempted to end the madness. It took a few minutes, but we were finally able to get everyone under control. The men were nuts.

"Let's get out of here," Charlie said as he and Brian walked out toward the van.

"Wayne, one more thing before I go. Where were those Stone Saviors located in the story?" I asked him.

"Shīzāzuparesu," he said.

"Huh?" I said confused. He held up his finger to wait one minute. He pulled out a pencil and a small sheet of paper. I watched him scribble something on the sheet and then hand it to me. I quickly looked at the paper and it read:

シーザーズパレス

"What the hell is this?" I asked him.

"That's the symbol for the Stone Saviors' base," he replied.

"What does it mean?"

"I don't know. It could just be a cool drawing," he said laughing.

"Jesus, you're useless." Frustrated, I crumpled up the paper and put it in my right pocket. I then stormed out of the bar with Rick following behind.

Chapter Twenty-One

JACK COLSON

The birds chirped loudly, and the leaves cracked every time I stepped on them. The black work boots Paul had lent me were drenched along with my socks. It felt like I was walking in a puddle. Luckily, I had some clean clothes on. I'm not much of a flannel person, but the gray looked nice on me. The cotton was so soft pressed against my skin. Unfortunately, his khaki pants didn't fit as well. I had to wear a belt or else the pants were going to fall to my ankles. His pants were also baggy around the leg area. He may be smart, but he could use some style advice. He dressed like he's Rob Schneider in the movie *The Waterboy*. A scruffy hunter for short.

"So where are we going anyway?" I asked Paul.

"Well...outside of admiring the great view, I thought we could do a little hunting," he replied.

"Hunting? I've never held a gun before. I can't hunt," I said loudly.

"What, your father never took you hunting?" he said chuckling. I put my head down and didn't say anything for a few seconds.

"I, uh…I've never met my father. He left when I was very young. I was raised by my mom," I responded sadly.

"Oh, I'm sorry to hear that. It must have been difficult," he said.

"You'd think, but I'm an only child. I can fend for myself," I said laughing.

"Ah, a boy that's independent. That's always a plus. I had a son too, you know," he said.

"Oh really? What's his name?" I asked.

"I don't really like to delve into the details. We used to have a good relationship, but now we aren't on speaking terms. It's a shame. He had so much potential and then-" he stopped.

"And then what?" I asked.

"His ego got the best of him, and his old self was primarily forgotten," he replied.

"Oh," I responded as I sighed sadly.

"Well, let's begin to hunt. It's our male time without Ava right now," he said.

He pulled out a large hunting rifle from an oversized bag he had thrust over his shoulder. It had an impressive scope and was black with gray lines all over. It almost looked like the rifle was covered in spider webs, but I quickly realized that it was just the design. The gun was pointed at the ground. He slowly lifted the gun up into the air and listened to the birds chirping above us. He slowly placed his finger on the trigger and...BANG!

The bird slowly dropped a hundred feet out of the air. Its body hit the dirt, and the leaves flew into the air around it. The bird was silent. Motionless. Lifeless.

"Well, your turn," Paul said. I looked at him confused.

"I don't know how," I said.

"I'll show you; it's not that difficult. First, you need to put the butt plate, or the back of the gun, in a place called the shoulder pocket. It's just under your collarbone and left of your right shoulder. That's if you're righthanded. Are you righthanded?" he asked.

"Yeah, I am," I replied.

"Okay good. Now, all you need to do is point your left shoulder at the target, place your left hand on the forestock for some support. It's a little further than the scope, but it should give you more control. Lastly, squeeze the trigger until the gun fires. Simple," he said.

He handed me the gun, and I began to lift it up toward him.

"Whoa, whoa. Another rule about guns. Don't point them in the air at someone you don't want to get hurt. It's dangerous," he said.

"Okay," I responded. I placed the butt plate of the rifle in the "shoulder pocket," grabbed the forestock with my left hand, and pointed the gun at the ground. I looked up to see a few birds flying around above us. I slowly raised the gun above my head. I looked through the scope and fired. The gun kicked back hard, and it hurt my shoulder. I wasn't expecting it.

"Well, not bad for your first attempt. You almost got one of them," Paul said, chuckling.

"I didn't even see the bullet," I said as my face lit up with confusion.

"A few more shots, and you'll start to see it. It's a feeling. You need to be confident that you are going to hit the target. It's like playing a sport. You cannot expect to guard your opponent if you believe he's better than you. You're just psyching yourself out. Now give it another go," he replied.

"Alright, I'll try," I said. I lifted my gun up once again and scanned the sky. There was nothing but the puffy white cumulus clouds and the blue in the sky. I tried to listen for birds. I heard nothing. I watched the trees dance and the leaves drop to the dirt. I had tunnel vision. I was laser focused. I kept swinging my head around and around and around and a-

"Jack, there's no more birds. We'll see if we can catch them on the way back," Paul said loudly. I got distracted. I was in a daze or something.

"Okay," I replied as we began to head back. We walked back

to the cabin silently, and I looked over at Paul.

"I thought you were going to help me begin my training? I want to know everything there is to know about the ice gem. I need to be prepared to fight the S.O.A.S. if they do come after me," I said.

"You have begun your training. Patience...relaxation and confidence are the key elements to remember when confronted with fear. Only then will you truly be able to harness your abilities and reach the highest potential of your powers," he said.

Chapter Twenty-Two

Liam Scarr

"Well this is just great!" I screamed as I crumpled up the small sheet of paper and tossed it in the garbage. I threw myself onto one of the metal chairs, lifted my black boots up on the metal table, and looked around at our empty apartment. I aggressively fixed my messy collar on my short sleeve, button-down shirt, and then proceeded to use the palms of my hands to slick back the sides of my hair. I looked around at the empty apartment. Rick and Charlie were nowhere in sight, but the kid stood in front of me eager to take action.

"What are you looking at me for? I did all I could. You're lucky I helped you get this far. You know the only reason I'm even looking for your friend is because this stone is quite important. But now...now it's starting to become more difficult by the second, and I don't know if this gem is worth our little expedition," I said with my snarky demeanor as I shot up and paced around the room.

"What did the sheet even say?" Brian asked.

"What's it to you kid? I said it was nothing. Are you some

type of mind reader?" I replied sarcastically.

"I just want to know. Maybe it's in a different language or a code or something else," he said eagerly.

"I doubt it," I responded.

"Well, why don't you just let me see and maybe we can-"

"Enough!" I screamed, interrupting him. He stared at me angrily as we both looked into each other's eyes in silence. I was looking at him for so long, it felt as if I could see right through him. Inside him.

"If your friend didn't leave you behind, you wouldn't be stuck with us," I said.

"He didn't leave me," he replied.

"Ooooh, I see. You let your friend go off on a little adventure, and you thought it was idiotic so you uh...decided not to run?" I said laughing.

"Yes, that's exactly what I did," he responded.

"A piece of advice...always support your partners, or in your case your friend. I know you think I'm a bad guy because I rob banks and kill people occasionally, but we're not as different as you think," I stated as I walked around him in a circle. He stared at me confused. He was a deer in the headlights. Clueless.

"We are not similar in the slightest. I don't kill people. I don't rob banks. I don't break the law. I'm not similar to a...a...a thug!" he shouted pointing at me.

"So that's what you think of me? Well, guess what? I may be a thug, but I didn't let my friend leave me because he was trying to save a foolish stone!" I said as my face was almost touching Brian's. After a few seconds, he stepped back and then turned away. I walked toward the fridge and grabbed a bottle of Coke. I screwed the bottle cap off and threw it onto the cold floor. I then turned my head as I proceeded to return to my metal chair, plopping my black boots back on top of the table.

Rick and Charlie entered the room. They both walked toward me as Rick took a seat to my left and Charlie took a seat to my right.

"That kid is a nuisance," I said quietly.

"I could take care of him," Rick replied.

"Jesus Rick, he's just a kid. I don't think Scarr wants him dead," Charlie stated.

"It would certainly make things a lot easier," I said, chuckling. Charlie's eyes lit up in amazement.

"What's wrong with you? You don't want him dead. I know you want that stone," Charlie replied.

"I do, but I don't need the kid's help. He's been going on to me about how he wants to see the note Wayne gave me. He believes it has some sort of hidden meaning that I didn't seem to notice. Possibly another language or something," I told him.

"Well, the urban legend of the Power of Four supposedly originated in Japan, so there's always a possibility," he said.

"Japan? Alright, we'll take another look then," I said eagerly. I lifted myself out of the chair as I quickly walked toward the garbage can. I looked inside at all the aluminum cans and leftover food. I reached my hand inside and grasped the small sheet of paper. I instantly scanned the sheet to verify it was the correct one, and it was. I sat back down at the table and placed the paper on the table. Both Rick and Charlie examined the paper attempting to comprehend its meaning.

"So is it Japanese?" Rick asked.

"I believe so. We'll find out right now," Charlie said as he pulled out his phone. He searched Google translate as he then began to enter the symbols. Once he finished typing all of the symbols on the paper, the English translation read "Caesars Palace."

"Brian!" I yelled.

Brian walked through the door a few feet from us. He slowly proceeded to walk toward us, and we showed him the hidden meaning of the writing on the paper. He examined the Google translate words in silence, and his brain zoned in. His thoughts filled the air as he came to a conclusion.

"So we need to go to Caesars Palace in Las Vegas," he concluded.

"What makes you think you're calling the shots kid? I thought we just agreed to take care of him?" Rick looked around at us..

"I wouldn't exactly call it an agreement," Charlie said.

"So are we going to kill him or not?" Rick screamed. Brian stood there shivering in fear. His face was perfectly still as he attempted to not make a sound.

"Why are we always deciding to just kill people automatically?" Charlie replied.

"Cause we're criminals," Rick mumbled in his deep voice.

"Hey, everyone listen up alright? The kid's right. This stone wants to go to someplace safe, and this is the best lead we've had, so everyone stop screaming at each other and pack your things. We're going to Vegas!"

Brian, Charlie, and Rick all stared at me in silence as I began to walk away from the group.

Chapter Twenty-Three

Austen Wolf

I sat down in my lab and stared into space. I held Jack Colson's personal file in my hand as I examined every page of it. Two of my business associates walked through the doors of my lab, waiting for me to acknowledge their presence.

"What is it?" I asked.

"Special Agent Diaz has just finished interrogating Dylan Kennedy. He provided very little information about the teenagers. However, he has gotten word from a reliable source who claims he knows Liam Scarr's whereabouts," one of the associates replied.

"Good. Let's keep this information a secret. We don't want any of the other scientists in the POE Labs to get the wrong idea about our investigation," I told them.

"Of course," they said.

I stood up, left my lab, and walked down the hall to the elevator. My office is on the tenth floor of POE Labs, which is the top floor. I took the elevator to the sixth floor where I walked down a small hallway leading to an open room where I could see the masterpiece. The room was extremely large, and the ceiling was probably fifty feet high. The room was filled with scientists as they all surrounded the structure in the middle of the room. It was beautiful. It was a large, spacious tube standing up like a person. The tube was mostly clear with slight shades of blue on the sides. There was a clear door to enter the tube large enough for a human being to fit through. The tube was twenty feet high with two large metal beams sticking out the top. The beams were probably ten feet long allowing the structure to look like the letter Y. Two large metal spheres were connected to the ends of the metal beams, and it was clear that they enabled the device to have some sort of magnetic field around it when activated. One of the scientists began to approach me. He wore a white lab coat with a gray sweater underneath and jeans. His hair was short and neatly combed to the right. His glasses took up half his face.

"Mr. Wolfe, it's great to finally meet you. My name is Dan Slater, and I'm the head physicist in charge of creating a device that can reach absolute zero," he said.

"Yes, it's nice to meet you," I said as I shook his hand and put on a nice act for him.

"I wanted to inform you that we have made great progress with the construction of the device. The structure is built, but we haven't constructed the laser yet. We are still figuring out how exactly to build a laser with enough intensity to reach absolute zero. Once we are able to figure out how exactly to do that, then it should be a very simple process to successfully operate the Doppler laser cooling device. Hopefully, the device will be done in a few months' time," he said.

My eye widened. "A few months?" I screamed. I looked down at the scrawny scientist.

"Mr. Wolfe, no one has successfully created a device that could reach absolute zero. This would be a huge step for the world of physics. I have my best team of scientists trying thousands of different formulas and attempting to formulate alternate solutions. We are only human, and it isn't physically possible to have a device of this caliber done before a few months' time," Dan replied. I looked at him with disappointment.

"Professor, I'm a busy man, and I need my business to be taken care of as quickly as possible. I'm on the cusp of achieving a power out of this world once I gain control of the ice gem and the death stone. A lot of people are trying to stand in my way, but they won't stop me. We won't have much time to wait for this device to be completed after I have control of the ice gem. It would only be a matter of time before Ava is able to overpower me if I don't separate her from the ice gem. I picked you for a reason. The reason being that you are extremely intelligent and have vast amounts of knowledge regarding Doppler laser cooling. But you're not one of a kind. You can be replaced within seconds. I suggest you and your group of scientists triple your efforts to complete this device within two week's time at most. I better see a significant amount of progress the next time I return, or a paycheck won't be the only thing you're going home without," I said as I stared at him angrily. I heard him swallow loudly as he looked away from me.

"I understand. We will triple our efforts," he replied nervously.

"Good. I'm glad we are on the same page," I said. I left the room as the doors shut behind me.

Chapter Twenty-Four

Jack Colson

I sat on the couch and watched Paul walking toward me. He was holding the ice gem in his hand and proceeded to give it to me.

"There is something you must know about the Power of Four. It is the most difficult aspect of destroying all four stones. No stone can be destroyed until the Farisphonite, in this case Ava, is extracted from the stone. The Farisphonite Miya Hart who has vowed her life to protecting the death stone is the only Farisphonite who has opted to protect the stone by living outside of it. The other three Farisphonites all lived inside the stone. Once the stone reaches what's called the 'tipping point,' then the Farisphonite will be extracted from the stone. All you need to know is that the ice gem's tipping point is absolute zero. Despite the fact that this temperature is extremely hard to achieve, you must ensure that Ava is never exposed to that temperature. Do you understand?" he said.

"Yes. I understand," I replied.

"Good, stand up. It's time for your second lesson," he said. I instantly stood up and followed him onto his porch. He sat down in a rocking chair, and I sat down on a wooden chair next to him.

"I brought you out shooting the other day to teach you how the ice gem works," he said.

"What do you mean?" I asked.

"Just as you point a gun at a target, you point the ice gem at a target. The only difference is that guns shoot bullets, and the ice gem shoots out cold air allowing it to freeze objects and even people," he said as he leaned toward me. "Your N plus bloodline is rare, and it's important that you don't forget that," he said as I nodded. "Have you experienced any side effects of using the ice gem?" he asked curiously.

"No. Not really," I replied. I began shivering a little bit as I suddenly realized that it became extremely cold.

"What do you mean not really?" he asked.

"Well, I did experience an extremely bad headache the night after I found her, but that could have been from a hangover," I said.

"That is certainly a side effect of using the ice gem," he said as stared at me closely for a minute.

"Are you shaking?' he asked.

"Yeah, it's really cold outside right now."

"It's seventy degrees outside and sunny," he replied. I looked at him confused before looking at all our surroundings. The

sun was blaring down on us, and Paul was even sweating
a little.

"Why am I so cold?" I asked myself. I looked back at Paul,
and he chuckled.

"What's happening to me?" I asked concerned.

"Relax. You must remain calm. This is common for
someone in your shoes. When you discovered Ava, she latched
onto you. The next day you experienced a massive headache
since your body encountered nykrons, which are particles that
your body does not recognize. In order to establish themselves
as a known particle, they rush toward the brain, which is why
you experienced a strong headache. That was the first phase.
The second phase you're experiencing now before my very
eyes. Sudden bursts of cold air. It's warm outside, but you feel
as if it is cold. Why? Because at this point you have been with
Ava long enough that thousands of nykrons have entered
your body. These nykrons come from the ice gem, so they
are extremely cold, and they need your body to cool down in
order for them to form a home there," he said.

"Is this the last phase?" I asked.

"There is one more phase. Phase Three. The longer the
bond between you and Ava lasts, the more powers from
the ice gem you will soon be able to use. However, using
powers without Ava's help can cause dizziness and loss of

consciousness. Using your powers without the help of Ava makes you lose nykrons. This will make you weaker. If you do not make physical contact with Ava after this, you risk losing all your nykrons which will inevitably kill both you and Ava."

I looked at Paul nervously.

"Well, there has to be some sort of way that I could cope with these phases. How can I stop these cold bursts from happening?" I asked.

"I have an idea," Paul said. He ran inside for a minute, and when he came back out, he was holding a diamond-shaped crystal amulet.

"Okay...relax in your chair, and watch the amulet," he said as he swung it back and forth like a pendulum. I examined it intently.

"Hold the ice gem out in front of you...feel it in your hand. Its crystals. Its cold temperature....Visualize yourself in that climate, and trust that Ava will guide you through it. Do you trust her?" he asked.

"I do," I replied.

"And on the count of three you will sink into your chair. One...two...three," he said.

My eyes opened, and I was lying in a few inches of snow. I looked around, and there was nothing. Just snow. It looked like it was cold outside, but to me it felt like I was walking on the beach.

"Hello!" I shouted

"Hello," Ava said. I looked around, but I didn't see the ice gem.

"Where are we?" I asked.

"You are inside the ice gem," she replied.

"What? How? How do I get out?" I said.

"You have to embrace the cold. You can't leave the stone until you become one with the cold climate. It must be a part of who you are. A part of your being," she replied. I looked around confused.

"How do I do that?" I asked. I looked around, but there was no response. I began to walk around in search of anything until a twenty-foot icicle landed a few feet in front of me. I instantly jumped back as I fell down into the snow.

"What the-!" I shouted as I stood up and examined the incredibly large icicle. I could see my reflection in the icicle and suddenly it changed into Paul's face.

"Paul?" I said surprisingly.

"You must prove that you're one of them," he said.

"One of them?" I asked.

BANG! BANG! BANG!

I turned around and three more icicles crashed forming the shape of a diamond around me. I looked up and saw another one falling from the sky heading directly toward me. I quickly jumped out of the way and started sprinting.

"What's going on? Ava...Paul! I need help!" I shouted. More icicles began to fall from the sky. One, then another, then two at a time, and eventually upwards of twenty at a time. I continued sprinting to avoid the falling icicles, but there was nowhere to run, nowhere to duck for cover. It was all open for miles. I began to breathe heavily as I started to get tired. I wanted to slow down, but I knew I couldn't.

"You're in the ice gem. Use its powers. Pretend like you're using me," Ava said.

I slowed down for a second and pretended I was gripping Ava in my hands. I held them up in the air as I tried to act like I was pointing Ava at one of the icicles falling from the sky. But it didn't work. Nothing shot out. No blue beam. The icicles started to fall closer to me, so I continued running. I was out of options. An icicle landed a foot in front of me, and I fell to the ground. I crawled backward as another icicle landed inches away from my head. I grabbed the large icicle in front of me and held onto it. I pressed both hands against it.

"I need the ice gem. I don't have powers," I said as I fully extended my arms.

The icicle split into a billion pieces. I looked at it in shock. I looked up at the sky, and there were no more icicles falling. I smiled in relief that I wasn't crushed to death. All the icicles slowly began sinking into the snow. Soon enough, it was just me again. I took one step forward, and I sunk into the stone.

"Release," Paul said as I jumped back in the wooden chair I was sitting in, realizing that I was back at Paul's cabin. I lifted up the ice gem and looked at it closely. I suddenly noticed I wasn't cold anymore. I was warm. I was actually sweating.

"You did good kid," Paul said as he walked toward me and patted me on the shoulder. I placed Ava on my lap as I rubbed my face in relief that my second lesson was finally over.

Chapter Twenty-Five

Austen Wolfe

We had completed our final descent. The plane was on the runway and soon came to a complete stop. Violet and I walked off the plane and over to a small black Lincoln. One of my drivers was in the front seat.

"Where to?" he asked.

"Brookfield," I responded. Once we arrived, I realized that Brookfield was an extremely nice city. The buildings were all made of brick that reached toward the sky.

I opened my car door as I stood up and stretched out my back. I looked to my right, and Violet was signaling for the agents to come toward her. Ten agents came out of the two pickup trucks that pulled up behind the Lincoln.

"Scan every inch of this forest until you find the ice gem. If you come across any stragglers, don't kill them. Set your guns for stun, and contact me immediately. I will not accept failure. The longer the ice gem is out of our hands, the bigger threat it becomes. Ava is extremely powerful. Do not underestimate her abilities or her potential allies if there are any. Now get moving," I said.

They all began sprinting through the woods behind the warehouse. Their rifles were up and ready, their eyes wide as they scoped out their prey like wolves. They stayed in small packs as they split up hoping to cover every piece of the forest. There was nothing in sight though. Only the trees, the leaves, and what we had on our backs.

Unlike the other agents, Violet wasn't dressed in a black suit. She wore black boots accompanied with black shorts. She had on a clean, tight, dark purple short sleeve shirt. On her left hand she had a few bracelets. However, on her right hand she wore a wrist rocket. She carried two purple Chiappa Rhino revolvers, and she had a holster on each leg. I had a nice gun, too. A gold revolver. The gun didn't have a scratch on it. It glistened in the sunlight.

"Violet," I said.

"Yes, Mr. Wolfe?" she replied.

"You can call me Austen. You don't need to be so formal," I replied as I chuckled.

"Okay...Austen. What are we looking for?" she asked.

"The ice gem is what we seek—mystical artifact with blue crystals. You are the expert in geographical terrain. We need your help in pinpointing its precise location. The stone is very dangerous in the wrong hands."

"What is so important about the stone?" she asked eagerly.

"The stone has special abilities, and it needs to be contained. We can't have a weapon of this caliber floating around the streets. It must be contained, and with your help we shall have no problem doing so. All we want is the stone. The teenager and his friends will be unharmed," I said blatantly lying to her face.

"Okay, I will round up a group of my best troops, and I'll lead the search party in the woods," she replied.

"I admire your leadership and eagerness to aid our search for the stone. However, I will be leading the search party through the woods. You will be more of a commander rather than the captain," I told her.

She stared at me intently before storming off into the woods behind the other agents. I could tell she was angry at me, but I didn't care. This was my mission, not hers. The tension grew as she turned around and looked at me, but we quickly broke eye contact and began to walk through the woods. She followed my lead for what felt like a day, but in reality, it was only a few hours. The only sound that was produced was the crackling of the leaves on the ground. No voices at all.

Chapter Twenty-Six

Liam Scarr

I laid back on the soft black couch in our apartment. The television was playing the movie *The Dark Knight*. Rick was sitting next to me, watching the movie intently. I pulled out my Desert Eagle pistol from my holster and slowly began to clean it with the white handkerchief I pulled out of my pocket. I rested my black boots on the small table in front of the couch. Rick and I sat there in silence for a minute or two before Charlie and Brian walked into the room.

"Great movie," Charlie said as he quickly poked his head in front of the television.

"Yeah, nothing better than watching a movie about a psychopath," Rick said as he chuckled. Brian looked at us nervously for a second before putting his head down and walking into another room. I watched him slowly walk into one of the bedrooms and close the door behind him. Charlie grabbed one of the metal chairs from the kitchen table, dragged it next to the couch, and sat down.

"So we're leaving for Vegas tomorrow afternoon?" Charlie asked.

"Yeah. Last night in this apartment. We got all our supplies ready?" Rick mumbled.

"It seems like we're carrying too much weight," I said rudely. Rick and Charlie both looked at me confused.

"What do you mean boss?" Rick asked. I quickly stopped cleaning my gun as I planted my black boots on the rug below us. I put my handkerchief in my pocket and my gun back in my holster. I slowly leaned forward as I rested both my elbows on my knees. I touched my fingertips together as I looked at both Charlie and Rick.

"The kid," I said snarkily.

"What's wrong with the kid?" Charlie asked.

"He's been with us a while. A little too long," Rick mumbled.

"He's not a burden to bring along," Charlie replied.

"I didn't sign up to help a lost dog find its bone. It's not my problem," I said.

"So how did you want to handle it then?" Charlie asked concerned. I stared at him in silence for a few moments before Charlie stood up.

"I'll kill him," Rick mumbled as he bounced up from the couch and proceeded to walk toward the room Brian was in.

"Hey!" Charlie said loudly as he ran toward him. Charlie got within a few feet of Rick, and Charlie was given the look.

Rick stared into Charlie's eyes like a monster. Like an animal. It was clear that Charlie wouldn't stand a chance against Rick, but for his size he'd put up a good fight.

"Don't get any closer," Rick mumbled to Charlie in his deep voice. Luckily, Charlie listened. I instantly stood up from the couch and turned around.

"Rick, take it easy," I said, trying to calm the situation. Rick turned around and looked at me in a fit of rage.

"You're not the boss of me-"

"Actually, I am," I said, interrupting him.

"I was just about to handle the situation."

"Not like this. Not you. You're in an idiotic rage and don't think about the repercussions of your actions. You're a maniac just like the Joker. A loose cannon just waiting to blow. We'll handle it my way," I said. Brian came out of his room and looked at all three of us confused.

"I'll do it," Charlie blurted out as he walked over to Brian and signaled for him to follow. Brian looked at us in fear as he had no choice but to follow Charlie. I watched Charlie grab his gun as they both left the apartment. Rick still stared at me angrily.

"If that's how you feel about me, then why haven't you taken me out? Huh?" Rick asked angrily. I stood there silently as I rested my hand on my holster.

"You ain't got the guts," Rick added as we both stared at each other until I took my hand off my holster and sat back down on the couch. Rick slowly began to walk over to the couch as he sat down next to me. We sat there together watching television for a few seconds before we heard a gunshot in the distance.

"Problem solved," I said.

CHAPTER TWENTY-SEVEN

JACK COLSON

The wind whooshed passed me as I cruised by the trees surrounding me. It was early morning, so the sun had just risen over the hills. I looked both ways and quickly realized I was a mile from Paul's cabin. I turned around to head back in the other direction when I heard a raspy call from a crow close by. I looked around and saw a crow swooping down toward a small nest resting on a tree branch only a few feet off the ground. There were nesting blue jays that were perfect for an early morning breakfast. I instantly sprinted toward the nest in order to scare the crow away. Luckily, I succeeded. The crow began to retreat and quickly flew off. I watched the nest for a second, noticing that there were five baby blue jays. Sensing danger, the mother flew into the nest in order to protect her five children. I smiled and then proceeded to continue my morning run.

Paul was waiting outside the cabin when I returned.

"How was the run?" Paul asked.

"Good. It helped clear my head," I replied.

"That's great. You haven't been experiencing any cold bursts now have you?"

"No. I've been good now."

"You're learning to utilize your abilities better now. Proving that you were able to destroy that icicle using your powers shows that you are gaining strength."

"I still am not exactly sure how I was able to destroy it."

"You proved you belong. Physically touching the icicle enabled you to unleash the powers that you share with Ava. However, you must be aware that your powers work a little differently than hers. You aren't capable of freezing objects like a gun. Only together you are given that ability. In order for you alone to freeze objects, you must lay your hands on the object and mentally envision the nykrons releasing themselves from your body. But remember the dangers of using your powers in the absence of Ava. You'll be releasing nykrons from your body, and they will continue to leave your body until you make physical contact with Ava. This will initially make you very weak, and you will risk your life and Ava's if you were to lose all of them," Paul said as he turned around and walked into the cabin.

I waited a minute before following him inside. He was standing in front of the couch and signaled for me to come over.

"Jack, sit down. It's time for lesson three," he said. Paul

walked over to his desk, picked up Ava, and handed her to me.

"It's imperative that you fully understand the powers and abilities of the ice gem since a few of them are shared between the two of you."

"I know that I can freeze things. Objects or people."

"Yes, but that is only one of the many powers. Another essential power is the use of a force field."

"A force field?"

"Yes. If needed, Ava can create a force field, but she needs to be in physical contact with you to do so."

"What other powers do I have?"

"In the situation that you and Ava are not together, Ava can transmit visual messages to you through the use of holograms that will appear on the palm of your hand."

"Wow! This is all uh...a lot to take in. I know it's important that I know all of Ava's abilities, but-"

"But what?" Paul asked.

"It's not using the powers that I'm afraid of. I mean I've used some already. I'm just scared that I'm not strong enough to protect Ava from the S.O.A.S.," I said.

"You are," Ava replied.

"But I'm not! I mean...I'm nothing more than a teenager. I can't take on the S.O.A.S. by myself," I said as I stood up. Paul began to pace back and forth as he rubbed his chin.

"Your fears are consuming you, but you must face them. Luckily, Ava can help you with that. You best sit down to hear this," Paul said. I noticed the ice gem began to glow brightly in my hand, which was odd.

I slowly sat down on the couch, and I continued to sink into the cushions. I didn't stop, and after a few seconds my feet landed on the edge of a cliff. My feet wobbled as it was clear that the rocks were not entirely stable. I was looking down at a raging river which appeared to be thousands of feet below me. My eyes lit up as I slowly began to back away from the edge without losing my footing. I tried to grab onto a tree branch above me, but it broke off in my hands. I was frightened to death. I had never experienced this much fear. My hands were shaking, and my head was pounding as I attempted to comprehend what was happening.

"End of the line!" a man screamed. I turned around to see a middle-aged man dressed in a black suit. He wore a red button-down shirt underneath with a black tie. He was holding a gold revolver which he pointed directly at me, causing my body to shift into overdrive. I felt a different type of fear that I couldn't recognize. I didn't know who this was, but I was petrified of him. He walked toward me, and I took a step back causing me to almost lose my balance. The rocks wobbled under me, and it was distressing how close I was standing to the edge of the cliff.

"Who are you?" I asked.

"You don't recognize me? I'm Austen Wolfe," he said as my eyes lit up.

"I've heard a lot about you," I said.

"Good. Then you realize it is useless to try and stop me in my quest to achieve the Power of Four. Before you get yourself killed, I suggest that you hand over the ice gem," he said. I looked at him confused before reaching into my pocket and pulling out the ice gem.

"Yes. That's it," he said as he held out his other hand. "Toss it here," he said.

I looked at him and then behind me in silence. I took a deep breath and stood up straight. My hands stopped shaking as I stared at him confidently.

"Never. I'll never give it to you...you failed Mr. Wolfe. I'm not afraid of you, and I'll do whatever it takes to protect Ava," I said. He looked at me defiantly.

"I'll take it by force then."

"You can try," I said as I turned around and leaped off the cliff.

Chapter Twenty-Eight

LIAM SCARR

"Let's go. The more time we spend here, the more time the stone is on the streets at risk of being taken by someone who isn't us," I said. Charlie ran over as he tossed a few bags in the back of the Blue Mystique.

"Are we all ready?" I asked.

"I think so," Charlie responded, however, Rick didn't hear me. I swung the door open as I walked back into the apartment. Rick and Charlie followed me as we all sat down at the metal table.

"Hey Charlie, go finish putting all our bags in the van while me and Rick take our last look around the apartment. We got some business to discuss," I said.

"I'm on it, boss," he said.

"Perfect," I replied. I stood there and watched as Charlie quickly maneuvered over to the garage.

"What's this business?" Rick mumbled.

"Don't worry Rick, I just wanted to acknowledge your plan. I think it's good," I told him, smiling.

"What plan?" he replied.

"We just got rid of the kid, and maybe it's time to make our group even smaller," I said.

"Ooooh...that plan," he responded.

"Yes...that plan. I know Charlie is part of our crew, but we have half the members now. Charlie's the tech guy. He's soft. But us...we're not, and we won't let him take us down that path with him. I've been doing some thinking, and I've decided that if Las Vegas takes us nowhere..."

"I should kill him," Rick blurted out, interrupting me.

"Precisely," I said. We walked down the stairs as we followed the hallway leading to the main entrance of the building.

"Boss, you think it'll come to that?" Rick asked. I looked at him with a blank face. I wasn't exactly sure if I wanted him dead if we didn't find the stone in Vegas.

"Only time will tell," I told Rick. He nodded. We continued walking down the hallway until we got to the door that led to the main entrance.

"This is the place. Everyone be ready," I heard a man's voice say on the other side of the door. I couldn't tell if the man was inside the building or just outside the main door, but wherever he was, he was close. I stopped immediately. Rick and I pressed our back against the wall and pulled out our weapons. We remained absolutely silent. I could hear multiple footsteps on the other side of the door. I listened for voices, but there were none.

"Which way?" a man's voice said.

"You five check every inch of this room while the rest of us will look in the basement," Agent Diaz said. Rick and I immediately sprinted to the end of the hall where there was actually some cover. Rick hid behind the left wall while I hid behind the right wall.

"Why are people looking through this apartment house?" Rick said angrily.

"A better question is who told these people that we were here?" I replied.

"It better not be the pigs," Rick said. The door busted down as two agents burst through. Gunshots filled the hallways hitting off the walls and the ceiling.

"Men in here! Men in here!" one of the men screamed.

"The FBI. Why is the FBI after us?" Rick mumbled furiously. Gunshots stopped from their side.

"Rick, hold your fire," I said. He stopped, and suddenly there were no more gunshots. I was extremely confused why they stopped firing at us.

"Liam Scarr," Agent Diaz called out.

"They know your name," Rick whispered to me.

"Liam Scarr. Is that you?" he said again.

"Who's asking?" I yelled back.

"My name is Agent Diaz. I am with the FBI. I was instructed by Austen Wolfe to find you. He wants to ask you a few questions about the ice gem," he said loudly.

"I don't know where it is if that's what you're asking, but I also don't take orders from anyone but myself!" I screamed as I fired a few shots at them.

"Have it your way!" he yelled down the hallway. I chuckled as I poked my head out and saw the man wearing a bulletproof vest with FBI inscribed on it. I quickly dove down the stairs to my right. I rolled down about ten stairs and landed right on my back dropping my pistol right beside me. Rick quickly fired a few returning shots as he bolted down the stairs. I leaped up and quickly grabbed my gun.

"I got one of them, boss!" Rick screamed.

"Agent Diaz?" I yelled.

"No, not him," he replied. Charlie came running out of the elevator quickly with his submachine gun in hand.

"Start the van!" I yelled at Charlie. I quickly flipped a folding chair around and threw it toward the agents. I heard multiple footsteps from the staircase as the agents unloaded on us. Rick and I ducked behind the dumpster which was about twenty feet from the main door leading to the parking lot. I fired a few shots, and knocked one of them down.

"Rick, cover me," I said. I quickly sprinted through the door into the parking lot as Rick laid a bullet into one of their men. The car finally started with Charlie already inside. I checked on the FBI's pursuit—they were getting close.

"Rick, now!" I shrieked. He bolted to the door but before he ran out the door, a bullet nicked his shoulder. He immediately grunted as he quickly grabbed it. He was clearly in some pain, however the bullet had just grazed him, so it was not in his body. I briefly saw the wound, and it was nothing major. Rick hopped in the van and laid down immediately. The FBI was now in dangerous territory. I fired a few quick shots, shut the door, and jumped in the back seat. In a matter of thirty seconds, the door opened just as Charlie made the turn out of the apartment complex parking lot. It was just enough time for us to make our escape.

CHAPTER TWENTY-NINE

SPECIAL AGENT DIAZ

The SUV zoomed down the street. I was sitting in the front seat while one of my agents was driving and the other was sitting in the back. I felt my phone vibrate in the pocket of my tan suit pants. I reached into my pocket and grabbed it to see who was on the other end. It was no surprise that it was the bureau. I quickly answered the phone.

"Agents Diaz here."

"Hi, uhh there's a teenager here who's requesting to speak with you," the woman replied.

"I wasn't expecting anyone. Did he tell you what it's regarding?" I asked.

"His name is Brian Shadow, and he says it's about something called the ice gem," she said, unsure if that was even a real thing. My eyes immediately lit up. I was speechless for a few seconds.

"If you don't want to talk to him, we can have another agent-"

"No, no, don't have him talk to anybody else. I'm on my way," I said before hanging up the phone.

The SUV pulled into a parking spot directly in front of the

building. The two other agents and I opened the car doors. We could hear the loud talking and the phones ringing from outside. It was clearly busy inside. I fixed my tan vest as I walked inside followed by the two other agents. They stopped a few feet behind me as I approached the woman at the front desk.

"Hi, I'm looking for Brian Shadow. He's here to see me," I said.

"Okay. I'll send him in," she replied.

"Thank you," I said as I walked into my office and sat down.

I waited a minute or two before a young man wearing grey khaki pants and a red polo shirt walked into my office. His clothes were sweaty and dirty. He wore glasses, and it was obvious he tried to fix his hair before coming here, but it didn't work too well. He seemed slightly drowsy and scared at the same time.

Surprisingly, it was really him. He was in Bermuda with Jack Colson and at the warehouse with the Red Sinners Gang. Now I was a little frightened why someone who I've been up against would randomly show up in my office.

"Please, sit," I said. Brian sat down and looked at me nervously. "Why are you here?" I asked.

"I wanted to speak with you about the ice gem. I know you searched Jack Colson's room in Bermuda," he replied.

"I did, and he didn't have anything," I said.

"I know because he gave it to me to hide. He found the ice gem in Bermuda in a series of caves called the Crystal and Fantasy Caves."

"You realize you just confessed to an obstruction of justice felony charge?"

"I know, and I'm really sorry. I didn't realize that at the time. I was just trying to help out my friend. I'm scared. I want to help Jack, but I can't. He's gone mad attempting to risk everything for this gem. I don't want to see him die trying to save some object."

"The only way I can help you with the charges you're facing is if you are willing to work with us to locate your friend as well as the ice gem."

"I will. As long as Jack isn't injured."

"He won't be. Trust me," I replied.

CHAPTER THIRTY

AUSTEN WOLFE

I headed down the hallway toward the elevator. The doors slid open for a second and closed after I entered. The elevator quickly dropped until we reached the sixth floor. I walked into the large room at the end of the hall and examined the many scientists standing around the absolute zero device in the center of the room. The structure looked similar to the last time I stopped by. There was still a gigantic tube in the middle of the room with a metal rod jutting out the top of it forming the shape of the letter Y. The metal spheres were still attached to the ends of the rod; however, the metal sphere looked double the size now. There was a large beam standing at about ten feet high. It had a large laser gun pointed directly at the tube. I walked toward Dan Slater and the few other scientists that were standing at a control panel about thirty feet away from the device.

"Have you figured out a way to intensify the laser enough so that an object inside the tube will reach absolute zero?" I asked.

"Yes, we doubled our efforts, possibly quadrupled them. We

were able to construct larger spheres at the ends of the rods in order to strengthen the magnetic field around the tube. We believe that this spherical shape is large enough to create a strong magnetic field that will still be stable. Once the laser hits the tubes, the stronger magnetic field should attract the atoms of the object toward the laser. An atom will then see its blue light shift which allows it to absorb that photon of light. This will slow the atom down, and it will move one of its electrons into an excited state. Once the atom is in its excited state, the atom will then re-emit a photon of light. Since the direction of an atom is random, there is no change in momentum which allows the atom to continuously absorb the photons of light and then re-emit them. Once all the atoms in the object are able to absorb and re-emit the photon of light from the laser, the object will reach zero degrees kelvin, negative 273.15 degrees Celsius or negative 459.67 degrees Fahrenheit—a state of absolute zero," he replied.

"I see. You have done well Professor Slater," I said.

"Thank you. It means a lot," he replied.

"Are you certain that it will work?" I asked.

"I'd bet my life on it. All our calculations are correct, and the structure is very well constructed. I have no doubt that everything will work perfectly," he said.

"And what do I need to know about starting it?" I asked.

"It's quite simple, actually. All you need to do is push a few buttons to turn on the magnetic field, and press that red button on the control panel to fire the laser," he replied. The other four scientists walked over to me and stood on my right while Slater stood on my left in front of the control panel. Each one of them walked up to me and gave me a firm handshake.

"A pleasure," each one of them said one after another.

Beep! Beep!

I reached into my pocket and pulled out my phone to see that Diaz was calling me.

"Hello," I said. I paused for a few moments. "I'll meet you up in my office," I replied as I headed to the elevator.

Diaz and a teenager walked into my office and sat down.

"This better be urgent," I said.

"It is. This is Brian Shadow. He's a close friend of Jack Colson and has agreed to help us in locating the ice gem," Agent Diaz replied. Brian shook my hand as he looked at me nervously.

"You look nervous," I said to Brian.

"No, I'm fine."

"Good...there's no reason to be. So tell me about Jack," I said.

"We grew up and went all through school together."

"What do you know about the ice gem?"

"Not much. I know Jack found her in Bermuda. I hid it in my room when Agent Diaz came to search his room," he said as I chuckled.

"When was the last time you saw the ice gem?"

"At Liam Scarr's warehouse. His gang kidnapped us off the beach in Bermuda. They didn't kill us though. They wanted to break the bond between Jack and Ava, but before they could, Agent Diaz showed up and Jack escaped with the ice gem."

"Where do you think they went?"

"I'm not sure but we can track him."

"How?"

"Using my phone. This app called Find My iPhone."

"Give it to me," I replied. Brian gave me a hesitant look.

"Agent Diaz said that if I agreed to help him that Jack wouldn't be harmed in any way," he said. I stared at Diaz for a minute before looking back at Brian.

"Absolutely. We wouldn't hurt him," I replied as Brian handed me his phone.

Chapter Thirty-One

Jack Colson

"So what's on the agenda for today?" I asked Ava.

"I don't know. Why don't you ask Paul?" she replied. I finished combing my wavy hair while staring at myself in the mirror and exited the room. I looked around his kitchen and living room, but he wasn't there, which was odd because he hung out in those rooms ninety percent of the time. I knocked on his bedroom door, but there was no answer.

"Paul....Paul?" I said loudly as I walked around the cabin. I heard a slight bang, but the sound came from below me. I suddenly felt a drop in my stomach because there was nothing below the cabin. I put my ear on the cold wooden floor, and I remained completely silent. I didn't hear anything until I heard a scraping sound as the rug flew up. I immediately jolted back and quickly stood up. It was a secret wooden door under the rug in the center of the living room. I sighed in relief as I saw Paul come out of the door.

"What's down there?" I asked.

"No time to explain that, but all you need to know is that you and Ava must hide now. Austen Wolfe is on his way here," he whispered.

"Now? How do you know?" I asked.

"I caught a quick glimpse of him on my morning walk and sprinted back here. He'll be here very soon, so pack a few things and hide," he said a tiny bit louder. I ran into my room and threw a few pairs of clothes into a backpack. I grabbed Ava as I sprinted into the kitchen, and Paul gave me a ton of water. He also handed me a rifle, and my eyes lit up. We both didn't say anything, so I zipped the bag up and quickly made sure I was ready to leave.

"Where should we..." I started, but I stopped after I heard a slight bang at the front door. Paul quickly guided me to his secret door under the rug as I quickly ran down the stairs.

"Go downstairs and find a place to hide. Once they leave, you must bring Ava to Caesars Palace in Las Vegas. There you'll find a group called the Stone Saviors who will help you protect Ava," he said quietly. I turned around to ask what he planned to do, but before I could say anything, the door was shut, and I could hear multiple footsteps above me.

The basement was dark with only a little bit of sunlight coming through the small windows. I walked around the basement; there were hundreds of cardboard boxes scattered around but very few places where we could hide. I held onto Ava tightly as I ducked down behind a clothes rack in the corner of the basement.

Chapter Thirty-Two

Austen Wolfe

The agents knocked on the cabin door hard. We tried to listen, but we couldn't hear anything. I gave them the signal, and the agents kicked the door in. The door slowly fell down into the cabin making a loud bang. The house was pretty empty with not that many pieces of furniture. This person only had the necessities.

"Look around, and tell me if you find anyone," I told them. I slowly followed behind them as Violet and I headed toward one of the bedrooms. We walked into a spacious neat room to find nothing. The ice gem was nowhere in sight, which immediately made me a bit frustrated.

"We found someone, boss!" one of the agents called out. I quickly turned my head as I walked into the living room. I entered the room, and my jaw dropped as I started to have flashbacks about my past.

"Why am I not surprised to see you here...PAUL?!" I screamed as he jumped.

"The pleasure's all mine," he said in his calming, old man voice. I squinted at him and began to slowly pace around him.

"So where's the ice gem?" I asked.

"What do you mean?" he said.

"Okay, okay, you want to do this the hard way I guess. How idiotic. Well let me tell you something...playtime is over now. I know the ice gem is here, and I'm gonna find it even if I have to tear this whole place apart," I said angrily. He looked at me silently as my men began tossing the cabin.

"The ice gem is not here," he said.

"Impossible...there's no way they escaped this quickly. Unless you somehow knew we were coming for whatever reason before we busted your door in, then it's physically impossible... impossible for the stone to have traveled so far that fast."

"Perhaps Ava just outsmarted you," Paul said as he smirked.

"Okay Mr. Jankins. You're talking to me. Austen Wolfe. I know all of your tricks, and there is only one thing I know for sure. There is a very dangerous weapon out on the streets which I intend to find," I said.

"A boy came in for an hour or two, but that was it. I didn't see no stone or this ice gem you speak of," Paul said, attempting to convince me that he was telling the truth. He may have my men fooled, but I could see Paul was lying right through his teeth.

"Liar!" I screamed, but before I could say anything else I heard a slight scratching at the sliding door behind us. I whipped my head around and saw the key to unlocking the truth about the ice gem.

"Oh it's just a dog…I'll let her in," Violet said. The dog sprinted in, and I signaled for my men to grab her. She looked petrified as the men circled around her. She growled loudly and began to attempt to swerve between us, but she failed.

"Owwww!" One of the men screamed as the dog bit his hand. The other men helped as they held her up like some sort of prize. Two men were enough to have the dog under control.

"What's her name?" I asked as I slowly petted Paul's dog. She attempted to bite me, so I jumped back quickly. I could tell she didn't like me very much.

"It's a he, and his name is Cooper," Paul replied.

"How interesting. Now, tell me where the ice gem is and who has it, or I'll burn the mutt to ash," I said loudly. Paul became nervous as he began to shiver, as he was uncertain of what to do. His lips moved but no words came out. I saw a few teardrops plummet from his eyes, however, he remained silent.

"Spit it out, or you're going to be spending money on an urn real fast," I said laughing.

"You can't kill his dog," Violet said as she walked over to me.

"Yes…I can," I replied quietly. She pulled out her gun and

held it to my head. The six agents surrounding us that weren't holding back the dog or Paul each aimed their rifles at Violet.

"Do you really want to try that?" I said.

"It's not the right way to handle this," she replied. I looked around and was able to make eye contact with one of my agents. I winked at him, and he nodded.

BAM!!!

Violet dropped instantly, and I could tell Paul was in shock.

"You killed her!" he screamed.

"Relax, she'll be fine. She's just been stunned," I said calmly. Paul didn't move as the agents dragged her closer to me. I looked him straight in the eye and my fist interrupted our staring contest. Paul's head dropped as the agents dragged him outside by his arms. The dog barked loudly and attempted to escape. The two agents wrestled with the dog, and luckily, they were able to restrain Cooper from escaping.

"Sir, what should we do with the dog?" one of the agents asked.

"Take him with us," I said. I checked around the house one more time and accidentally tripped over a strange hump under the rug in the living room. I looked down and began to feel the padding under the carpet. I grabbed the rug and the padding and lifted them up uncovering a secret trap door. I lifted up the door revealing a staircase leading to a secret room located underneath the house. It seemed to be much larger than an average basement would have been for this size house. I signaled for my men to come toward me, and we proceeded to walk down the narrow staircase that led to a dark room with tons of boxes piled up from floor to ceiling. I asked my men to bring down floodlights so we could easily search the entire room.

It was silent for a few minutes until I heard a gunshot. I looked around to see if any of my men had fired their weapons. They didn't.

One of the floodlights revealed Jack Colson holding a rifle with Ava resting on one of the cardboard boxes. Jack fired a few bullets as Ava fired a blue beam instantly freezing one of my men. My men quickly began firing shots back at them, and Ava was struck by one of the bullets. She ricocheted off the wall and landed on the ground. I quickly picked her up off the ground and put her in my pocket.

"Let's go! We have all we need!" I yelled as my men followed me up the stairs. Jack came out from behind the cardboard boxes but before he could do anything, I locked the trap door with Jack still down there. We then walked out of the cabin and headed back to Brookfield.

Chapter Thirty-Three

Austen Wolfe

Smoke filled the room as I watched the scientists gathered together in an attempt to fix the absolute zero device. Dan Slater was attempting to stop the smoke from coming out of the control panel, but his efforts were failing. He stared at Agent Diaz and I anxiously as he slowly walked toward us.

"Mr. Wolfe, I assure you we are doing our best to put an end to this problem. The absolute zero device should be operational in just a moment," he said nervously.

"I hope so, for your sake. We wouldn't want you delaying my plans," I said as I pulled back my suit jacket revealing my gold revolver. He stepped back alarmed and stood in front of me like a statue.

"Slater, we got it!" one of the scientists called out as we quickly realized that the smoke had stopped spewing out of the control panel. I pulled my jacket over my gold revolver as Dan Slater ran over and helped the other scientists set up the device.

"I heard you handled Violet," Diaz said.

"I didn't kill her, but let's just say she'll never disobey me again," I replied.

"That's good," he said.

"I believe your work here is done. I'll inform you if you serve any need to me in the near future."

"Thank you, Mr. Wolfe," he said as he left the room.

I slowly walked toward the absolute zero device. Once I reached the large tube, I opened the door and pulled out the ice gem from my pocket. I placed it on the chair in front of me and shut the door behind me. I looked through the clear tube at the ice gem.

"Ava," I said. I could hear her breathing heavily. She seemed frightened.

"Where am I? What am I inside of?" she screamed.

"You're in the POE Labs currently in a device that has the power to reach absolute zero. Once the process begins, you'll only have twenty-four hours before your body is extracted from the ice gem."

"That's impossible," she replied helplessly.

"It is hopeless to deny the truth. After the inside of the tube reaches absolute zero, you'll be extracted from the stone. With you out of the ice gem, there will be no more obstacles hindering my ability to destroy it."

"I won't let you destroy it!"

"Then you'll face the same fate as the other Farisphonites who shared the same belief as you do," I said as I walked to the control panel.

"Mr. Wolfe, the absolute zero device is fully operational. Should we start the cooling process?" Dan asked.

"Yes."

Dan and the other scientists began pushing numerous buttons on the control panel. I could see the magnetic field starting to form as bolts of energy shot from one large metal sphere to the other. One of the scientists readjusted the laser aimed at the tube.

"3...2...1...fire," Dan said as a laser beam shot out directly at the tube. The bolts of energy started moving fifty times faster as they shot in all different directions.

"AHHHH!" Ava screamed inside the tube.

"Easy now. Stabilize the magnetic field," Dan said as the other scientists messed around with a few of the buttons on the control panel. Suddenly, the bolts of energy began to move slower. "Perfect. The device has begun its cooling process successfully," he said.

"Good. Alert me when the cooling process is finished," I said as I headed toward the exit. All I could think about was Ava screaming and the fact that I was one step closer to achieving the Power of Four.

Chapter Thirty-Four

Jack Colson

banged on the door, but it didn't budge. I was trapped. I quickly scoured around looking for any way to help me escape this dark room, but there was nothing. The windows were too small to crawl through, and my rifle was out of bullets. I agonized in pain. It felt like I had been shot, but I realized it wasn't coming from me. It was coming from Ava. I could feel her pain as if I had been the one who had been shot. I could feel that the bond between us was growing immensely. It felt like I had lost someone that I couldn't live without. I was cold, hopeless, and scared. I was alone with nobody to help me now. I laid on the basement floor with the limited supplies I was given.

As the hours went by, I grew weaker and was still in pain. My supplies were running low, and I was in a daze from being locked in this basement for so long. I breathed heavily as I hoped I could just go back to my house in Brookfield.

"Why did I have to steal that stone in the first place?" I asked myself. I sat up, and it looked like I was staring in the mirror, but I wasn't. I looked like a blue ghostly figure. I looked at myself confused.

"Do you really wish you hadn't taken that stone?" the ghostly figure said.

"I wouldn't be locked in the basement right now if I hadn't," I said.

"I thought you were better than this. We're both better than this," he said.

"It's over. We lost," I said.

"We didn't lose. We just faced a challenge, and with that we must overcome it," he said.

"How? I don't have Ava or Paul. I'm useless without them."

"You don't think that. You're wrong, and I know you know it, too," he said.

I stared at my ghostly self as he slowly faded away. My eyes slowly began to close as I rested my head back onto the floor. I laid on the cold hard floor trying to get comfortable.

I heard a faint noise coming from upstairs. My eyes opened instantly. Using all my might, I pulled myself up off the floor and slowly crawled up the stairs. I banged on the door a few times as hard as I could. I waited a few seconds and listened, but I heard nothing, and the door didn't open. I laid on the stairs praying that someone would hear me and let me out. Then once again, I heard faint footsteps above me. I was about to give up all hope, but then I pressed the palm of my right hand against the door and waited a few seconds. I opened my eyes, but nothing happened. I did the same thing, expecting a different result, but once again, nothing.

I took a couple of deep breaths before trying one last time. I closed my eyes, focused, and put my hand on the door. When I opened them, the door was frozen solid. I looked at it and smiled as I rested on the stairs. I waited a few seconds...and it shattered like glass.

Liam Scarr, Rick, and Charlie were all standing at the top of the staircase.

CHAPTER THIRTY-FIVE

LIAM SCARR

Rick and I carried Jack by his hands and feet and put him into the back of the van. Jack woke up in a daze looking at all of us confused.

"What happened?" I asked.

"You were lying unconscious on the basement stairs," Rick said.

"How did you find me?" he asked.

"The energy power tracker had a very high reading in this area," I said.

"Wait, where's Brian?" he asked. Rick and I looked at each other.

"He's gone," I said rudely.

"What do you mean?" Jack said.

"He got caught in the line of fire...He's dead...I'm sorry." Charlie blurted out. Jack dropped his head in sadness for a few minutes before looking up at the rest of us. He looked at us tongue-tied, eager to get something off his chest.

"The S.O.A.S. They captured Paul and took the ice gem," Jack blurted out.

"Who's this Paul guy?" Rick asked.

"He knows a lot about the ice gem, and he was helping me learn more about my relationship with Ava," he said.

"Great. If you had listened to me then, we wouldn't be in this position. You should've let me hide the ice gem, and you should've gone back to living your boring teenage years without the stone," I said bluntly.

"Well, there's nothing we can do about that now. All we know is that we need to find Ava and Paul before the ice gem is destroyed," Jack said.

"Yeah, and how do you expect us to find them?" I replied.

Jack's hand began to turn light blue as a hologram of a large office building called the POE Labs appeared in his hand.

"What is that in your hand?" Rick asked.

"I believe it's Ava sending me some sort of layout of the building she's being held prisoner in," Jack replied.

"What's the POE Labs?" Charlie asked.

"The POE Labs," Jack responded. "It's a ten-story building with a basement located in Philadelphia, Pennsylvania. It is a part of the S.O.A.S. Organizational Complex. It is a research laboratory mostly related to physics and-"

"Alright, let's cut the lecture portion and get to the how to break in part," I said interrupting Jack.

"There are two main entry doors, one in the front and one

in the back of the building. Both doors require a POE Labs ID to enter the building," Jack replied.

"Alright, so how would we get an ID?" Rick asked. I rolled my eyes.

"We aren't getting an ID. First of all, we don't have a laminating machine that would be able to create a fake ID that would pass the system. We also don't want to take that approach because Austen Wolfe can identify all of us," I replied.

"What's the security system?" Rick asked.

"The building has an alarm system that will immediately go off if anyone without ID enters the building through the main doors or if any of the windows are opened," Jack said.

"It's like that bank in Old Lyme, ain't it boss?" Rick said.

"Exactly. Jack, where are the controls to the security system?" I asked.

He zoomed in on the hologram in his hand to a room right next to the back door on the first floor.

"The security system controls are located in the control room right next to the back door of the building on the first floor," he replied.

"So how do we break in? We can't get through those doors without an ID," Charlie said.

"Over the ten years the building has been standing, no one

has ever successfully broken into it," Jack said.

"I heard that one before," Rick mumbled.

"I don't need the recap of the break-in successes. I've never met a building that I haven't been able to break into in all my years of thieving," I said annoyed.

"Then how should we break in?" Jack asked.

"Alright, Charlie will handle the security system. He knows his way around high-tech security systems. There's always a flaw. He'll shut down the security system long enough so we can climb through the window of the tenth floor. If this Paul guy is so important, he's most likely being kept in Austen Wolfe's private lab on the tenth floor," I said.

"How do you know his lab is on the tenth floor?" Jack asked me. I laughed.

"It's basic power etiquette. If you own something, why wouldn't you want to be on the top floor? It's common sense that the people that work on the tenth floor of that building make the most money and have the most power in the lab. Besides that, I also used to work there," I said.

"I guess that makes sense, but how will we get to the tenth floor? We don't have a hook and ladder," Charlie replied.

"There is a series of ladders to the fire escape attached to the back of the building that allows you to climb from the street all the way to the roof of the lab," Jack said.

"Alright then, we'll find Paul and Ava and escape through the window. At least that's our plan on paper," I said. Rick and I chuckled as Jack looked at all of us confused.

"What does that mean, *it's our plan on paper?*" Jack asked.

"Kid, if I know one thing about breaking and entering, I know it's that things never go according to plan. We could have our timing down within seconds, but it doesn't matter. There's always something that we didn't account for, an unexpected guest or security system flaws that we haven't taken into account. I've been on a lot of heists, and it's all about improvising on the spot. Stick with me, and we'll be fine. We'll get your friend, and hopefully it'll be as easy as it sounds on paper," I said.

"I hope so," Jack replied.

"What's in it for us though?" I asked.

"What do you mean?" he asked.

"You don't expect us to risk our lives to help rescue your friends without some type of compensation," I said.

"After we rescue Paul and Ava, we can go to Caesars Palace in Las Vegas. A group called the Stone Saviors will reward you for helping save the ice gem."

"How much?" I asked.

"Two hundred thousand dollars," he replied

"It better not be a penny less than that," I said.

After a few hours, we reached the POE Labs. The building was all black with a hundred windows on every floor. I signaled for Charlie to park the car in the parking lot next to the POE Labs so that the trees would block the van.

"Alright, it's time," I said. Charlie grabbed his submachine gun and threw it over his shoulder. I handed Jack one of the Glock 22 guns in the back of the van. He put the gun in his pocket and stepped out of the van.

"You might not need it, but just in case," I said. Charlie grabbed the walkie talkies from the glove compartment. He attached one of them to the belt of his jeans and handed Rick and I one.

"Why do I need one?" Rick asked. "I'm going with Liam."

"No, you're not. You're lookout. You're staying in the van unless told otherwise. You're already wounded, so you'll slow us down," I told Rick. He stared at me angrily.

"You need my help. We're partners," Rick said.

"Yeah, and I would rather have my partner alive," I said. He stared at me angrily but in silence now. I nodded to Charlie as he ran out of the van. He looked both ways in the back parking lot, but nobody was in sight. He took a screwdriver out of his pocket and quickly unscrewed the four screws holding up the identification scanner. The scanner fell to the ground, and it took about two minutes for Charlie to rewire the system with ease. He screwed the scanner back onto the building and opened the door without the alarm sounding.

"We're all good. I'm inside. I'll have the security system down in a moment. You can begin your approach," Charlie said through the walkie talkie.

"Perfect," I replied. Jack and I ducked down next to the van and took a quick scan of the back parking lot. I grabbed the crowbar out of the back of the van and quickly ran toward the ladder. I looked behind me as Jack stumbled into the van, almost falling over.

"What the hell are you doing?" I whispered.

"I don't know what happened. I just didn't have any control of my body for a second," he said.

"Well, get a grip," I said sharply as he followed me to the ladder. I climbed up first followed by Jack, who appeared to be moving in slow motion. Once I reached the tenth floor, I was relieved that no one was in this lab. I hooked my arm around the ladder to stabilize myself and reached for the crowbar out of my back pocket. It took me about twenty seconds to open the window, and we both hopped into the room. The lab almost looked like a classroom. There were a few black lab tables around the room and a larger black lab table with a whiteboard behind it in the front. I quickly tip-toed over to the door and slowly closed it. We both ducked down out of the view of the working scientists.

"What now? How are we supposed to find out which lab he's in without being seen?" Jack whispered.

"We'll work fast," I replied. I slowly pulled the door open. I poked my head out to see if anyone was in the hall. I signaled for him to follow. We were on the far right-hand side of the hallway.

"Okay you scan the labs on the right side, and I'll take the labs on the left side," I said. He nodded. I quickly made my way down the hallway, peeking my head into empty rooms.

"Hey, Liam," Jack whispered, signaling me over.

"What is it?" I asked. He pointed to the lab right next to him. I looked through the window of the door, and I saw a dog inside but nothing else.

"I don't see anyone," I said.

"That dog is Paul's. Maybe he'll be able to sniff out where they are keeping him," Jack said.

"I didn't come here to save a dog. This is supposed to be an in and out task," I replied irritated.

"We can't just leave him in there," he said.

"You're willing to waste time on this mission to save some meaningless animal?" I replied angrily.

"The dog doesn't deserve to suffer," Jack said.

"Yeah, and I don't deserve to die for being some idiot do-gooder," I replied.

"I'm not leaving without him," Jack said demandingly.

I sighed and pulled out two lock picking devices made out of paper clips. I shoved one of them in the lock while I quickly slid the other paper clip in and out of the lock. I attempted to hit the pins just right so the door would open. Luckily, I had done this many times before, so it only took me a few seconds. The lock clicked, and the door opened.

"We're in," I whispered, but before I could finish my thought, the alarm sounded. Jack immediately ran in and grabbed the dog by the leash.

"Nice going Mr. Hero," I said to Jack.

"Boss, what happened?" Charlie said through the walkie.

"The kid's altruistic personality just screwed us. I'm done! I'm calling it off. We are getting out of here now!" I said to Charlie.

"I'm not going anywhere. We need to find Paul. We have to find Ava. We'll be able to take on a few agents, and the dog will quickly lead us to Paul," Jack said to me.

"Go find this Paul guy by yourself. I'm out. I didn't sign up to go up against a band of FBI agents again," I explained.

"Fine," Jack screamed as he ran toward the west staircase. I turned around and headed back toward the ladder on the other side of the hallway. I sprinted into the lab and grabbed my walkie talkie from my belt.

"Rick, the mission's a bust. I'm going down the ladder now before I get killed by an FBI Swat Team," I said to Rick through the walkie talkie.

"Boss, you can't leave that way," Rick replied.

"Why not?" I said. However, I didn't need an answer. I looked out the window and saw there were as many as ten agents standing by the back door of the building.

"There's a group of agents by the back door of the building," Rick reported in his deep voice.

"I'm going to the third floor. There's way too many of them scanning the ground floor," Charlie said over the speaker.

"I'll try to make it there. I'll see how far down I can go without being seen," I said as I sprinted out of the lab toward the east staircase.

Chapter Thirty-Six

Jack Colson

I jogged down the west staircase holding onto the railing until I heard multiple footsteps coming upstairs. I had cleared four floors before I had to stop on the sixth floor. I grabbed onto the wall gasping for air, almost falling to my knees. I fell into the door, and for a minute I didn't have the strength to open it. I realized what was going on, why I was so weak, and it terrified me. Something Paul said about the three phases of our relationship.

"Using your powers without the help of Ava makes you lose nykrons. This will make you weaker. If you do not make physical contact with Ava after this, you risk losing all your nykrons which will inevitably kill both you and Ava," I remembered Paul saying during the training.

Finally, I was able to open the door. The sixth floor had an extremely strange structure, like a tic tac toe board. There were all labs on the outer edges of the floor but in the middle of the rectangular floor were small unconnected pathways in both the horizontal and vertical directions leading to the other side of the floor. The pathways were about six feet wide and had a railing; they were only two feet off the ground. I looked down and I realized that the third, fourth, and fifth floors each had the same similar structure, however, each floor's tic tac toe board was rotated ninety degrees from the one above it. I guess the positive is that each of the four floors is rotated ninety degrees so that a person would only fall one floor down rather than four if someone were to fall over the railing. Cooper picked his head up and quickly looked down. Cooper's deafening bark hurt my ears along with the gunshots that came after. Bullets flew straight up in the air. A few agents were on the fourth floor attempting to shoot at me, but they had almost no angle because they were directly below me. I began to panic a little as I sprinted toward the other side of the floor. I attempted to fire some returning shots, but I didn't land any. I also practically had no angle. I darted around the sixth floor evading bullets and peeking into the room but there was still no sign of Paul. Two men broke through the staircase door and began to fire at me across the hall. I quickly ducked down. I sprinted toward the staircase door while Cooper sprinted past me and down the stairs. I tried to stop him, but I couldn't. I heard people coming up the stairs, so I was forced to close the door. I ran down a small narrow hallway that jutted out from the tic tac toe board. I was now out of the agents' line of sight. I practically couldn't keep my balance any longer. I was getting weaker by the minute.

"Jack," a whisper said. I looked around but I didn't see anyone.

"Jack," it said again, and I quickly recognized the voice.

"Ava," I said.

"Ja-" she said one last time only it was clear that the voice was getting weaker.

I quickly maneuvered toward a room at the end of the hall. I opened the door and didn't see anyone at first. I heard voices coming from the other side of the room, so I instantly dropped on all fours and crawled behind a metal octagon science table.

"Mr. Slater, the device has reached five degrees Kelvin," a man said.

"Good, only twelve more minutes before it hits absolute zero," Mr. Slater replied.

"Mr. Wolfe will be very pleased with our work," the man replied. I poked my head up to see two scientists standing next to a large control panel. There was a large beam standing about ten feet high directly next to them. It had a large laser gun that was shooting at the tube. They were both staring at a large object with a large clear tube that had two metal poles jutting out from the sides. The metal poles formed the shape of the letter Y and they each had metal spheres attached to the ends of them. There were electrical charges that moved between the two metal spheres. There was a clear door that led into the metal tube, and I quickly realized that Ava was inside of it. I could see on the timer that there were now only ten minutes left until the ice gem would reach absolute zero. I ran out from behind the table and pointed my gun at the scientists.

"STOP!" I shouted. They both jumped as they looked at me nervously.

"What do you want?" one of the men said.

"Turn it off. Turn it off now," I said.

"Okay, don't shoot. We'll turn it off," one of them said as he pressed a few buttons on the control panel that halted the electrical charges bouncing off the metal spheres. The laser beam disappeared.

I quickly ran over to the machine. I opened the clear door to the tube and grabbed Ava. It was like a sudden jolt of energy that ignited my shoulders to jump up as I felt my strength slowly come back to me. The ice gem was dim at first but now the light shone brighter than the sun.

We quickly made our way out of the laboratory and were immediately met by two agents entering the room. I held Ava out in front of me, and she was quickly able to freeze the two agents. I heard a number of agents coming up the stairs, so I headed toward one of the vertical platforms.

"I'm going to be surrounded in a matter of minutes," I thought to myself.

I continued sprinting until both staircase doors opened. Some men stopped on the sixth floor while I noticed some other men making their way above the sixth floor. There were probably five men on each side of the vertical platform. There were too many of them to attempt to shoot down or have Ava try to freeze. I would have been dead in seconds if I tested an FBI agent like that. I swiftly looked at the six-foot-wide platform, and I realized that there was nowhere to run, so I rapidly placed my gun in the pocket of my pants and took a leap of faith. I placed my hand on the mini railing and pushed off as my body floated in midair for a second until I roughly reached the fifth floor. I landed on my feet, but I stumbled and almost tripped over the railing which would have resulted in me landing on the fourth floor. I promptly regained my footing and glanced up at the agents above me.

"We got a runner. Fifth floor now!" one of them screamed.

I may have just jumped down a floor away from the agents, but I was still nervous. My heart pounded out of my chest as I realized that I was practically defenseless standing in the middle of the fifth-floor horizontal platform with a gun pointed directly at me. I thought that this was the end once I heard a gunshot or two. I grabbed Ava from my pocket and a bubble surrounded me—a blue, oval-shaped bubble. It was a force field.

"What do I do?" I asked Ava.

"Let's go find Paul. I can only hold this force field for a few minutes at most with all the gunshots coming our way," she said. I swung my head around and instantaneously went from zero to sixty in a matter of seconds. I kicked into second gear as I knew I had to escape the security agents. The force field disintegrated just as I reached the staircase.

"He's heading toward the lower floor!" one of the agents shouted over his walkie talkie. I rapidly froze a few agents in their tracks, but there were still more of them coming from the floor above. Bullets soared all around me. The agents were shooting a thousand bullets right through the middle of the staircase. I continued racing for my life, skipping two stairs every step I took to gain as much ground as possible in the short amount of time I had.

I was in full panic mode as I heard the door to the first floor open. I heard some gunshots below me, but surprisingly they weren't directed at me. It sounded like they came from below me. I prayed that there wouldn't be anybody on the first floor so I could escape. I reached it, and luckily someone had taken out a few agents, and they were lying on the staircase. I flung open the door but struggled to act as calmly as possible, even though I was being hunted down by an entire squad of agents. Luckily, my distance runner skills for the Brookfield track team allowed me to gain a somewhat comfortable cushion from the agents without even being that winded. I quickly turned right out of the staircase and headed down a large hallway and just turned into an empty lab and locked the door.

"What do I do? What do I do? What do I do?" I continued to ask myself. I examined the room, but there was nothing useful. The lab had a large table in the middle with a bunch of beakers, some cups full of water, safety goggles, and some labeled containers but nothing at all useful. There were a few windows, but my plan was not to escape. At least not yet. I attempted to feel around the walls and rapidly checked on the floor and under the table, but there was nothing.

"Ava, what do I do?" I asked her. I heard footsteps coming my way, so I knew I needed to come up with something fast. There was nowhere to hide, so I needed another way to leave the lab without using the door.

"The air vents above the lab table are the only other exit from this lab, which would allow you to still remain in the building," Ava replied.

"Alright, I got it," I replied nervously. I climbed onto the table knocking over all the beakers and water by my feet. The security force's footsteps began to get louder and louder. The vent was screwed on, so I instantaneously was out of ideas. I was surprised when Ava shot out cold air onto the vent blinds turning them into ice.

"Ava, what are you doing?" I whispered.

"It's ice now. The vent blinds should break very easily. Climb into the vent," she whispered back. I hit the vent blinds with my elbow, and they quickly shattered into millions of pieces like glass. I jumped up and grabbed onto the air duct and pulled myself up until my entire body was in the vent.

"What about the broken vent blinds? They'll know I'm in here," I said.

"Hopefully you'll leave the air duct before they notice," she replied as I slowly crawled through the vent so quietly that you could hear a pin drop.

Chapter Thirty-Seven

Austen Wolfe

Beep! Beep! Beep!

The blaring sound made my ears fall off as I immediately attempted to find out what was going on. I walked out of one of the first-floor conference rooms and I watched a few scientists walk past me as they began to head toward the front doors. I walked toward the lobby of the building where one of the security guards was at the front desk.

"What's going on?" I asked the security guard.

"It appears that someone triggered the alarm in your lab," he replied.

"My lab?" I asked angrily.

"Yes, it also appears that someone has shut off the security system, and we haven't been able to get it back up," he said.

"I want you to send a few men up to my office pronto, and I'll take a team of agents to check out the security system. Make sure all the other scientists evacuate the building immediately, and tell them to leave the premises for the rest of the day. I have a feeling who is behind this," I said clearly.

"Yes sir," he replied. He pulled out his walkie talkie and quickly ordered a security unit to check out the tenth floor while a few other agents should meet in the lobby with me to check out the security system.

I watched upwards of twenty agents make their way toward the east and west staircases. After a few minutes, about six agents came to the lobby and followed me down a long hallway. Once we reached the end of the hallway, we made a sharp left turn. I jogged toward the double doors at the end of the hallway as six agents followed me. We stopped about two feet before the door, and I signaled for one of the agents to open it. He whipped the door open, and we all dispersed. It was a large room with an enormous amount of wires on the wall. The room had a unique shape as it looked like two squares overlapping at the first square's top left corner. We were in a square room with a little V-shaped room jutting out from the left side. The room was steaming hot, and I quickly felt the heat. There was a large generator in front of us, so we were forced to split up. I went to the right as two agents followed, while the other four agents headed toward the left side of the generator. I looked around, but there was nothing unusual.

"Hey!" one of the agents shouted from the other side of the room, which was followed by a gunshot. I heard a body hit the floor, and I attempted to get a look at what happened, but someone had shot one of the pipes and smoke filled the room within seconds. Some of the agents on the other side of the room began to fire shots, but I wasn't able to see anything.

"I need some help fast!" someone screamed as the door flung open behind us. I coughed loudly as I attempted to find my way to the door as quickly as possible. I finally made it as the two agents behind me followed, and we tried to quickly catch our breath. I noticed two of the agents were about fifty feet ahead of us sprinting down the hallway firing shots at someone. We quickly followed them down the hall.

Bang! Bang! Bang!

A thousand bullets were flying all around the hallway. We turned the corner and watched as the two agents ahead of us were quickly gunned down by a man as they attempted to use the staircase door for cover. He began to head toward the main doors, but I pulled out my gold revolver and quickly blasted a fireball right at him. He ducked, and the fireball crushed the main doors as it knocked the man off his feet. I went into a full sprint down the hallway as I gained some ground. He was forced to make a right turn down at the lobby because he knew that he'd be susceptible to gunshots if he went outside. I was a cheetah as my legs moved as fast as possible. I was filled with rage, and I wasn't going to let this guy escape. I switched my gold revolver to the bullets setting before I dove toward the main lobby and fired two quick shots his way.

"Aaaaaaaah!" the man screamed as one of the bullets penetrated the back of his right thigh. He face-planted as he dropped his weapon. He was quickly able to enter one of the labs down the hall. He slowly grabbed his weapon as he attempted to get on his feet. He blindly fired about ten shots behind him taking out another one of my agents. He grabbed the doorknob and basically just collapsed into the lab. The only remaining agent and I sprinted toward the lab. We flung open the door and stormed into the room. We saw the man crawling on the ground as he was crying out in pain. He tossed his weapon away and rolled over on his back. He had his hand in the air as he saw two guns pointed at his face. His face was bright red, and his leg continued to bleed. I bent down on one knee so I could get close to him.

"What's your name?" I asked him.

"Charlie," he replied out of breath and clearly in a ton of pain.

"Where are your other friends?" I asked.

"What do you mean?" he asked. I looked at him stubbornly, and I pressed my thumb on his wound.

"Aaaaaaaaah!" he screamed in immediate pain. He reached

for his wound, but I grabbed his wrist with my other hand. I placed my gun right on his forehead and repeated the question.

"Where are your other friends?" I screamed.

"I don't know! I don't know! I swear! They were on the tenth floor the last I heard," he responded quickly in fear of making me angrier. I pushed him to the ground and stood up. Charlie reached for his leg as he was still in a great deal of pain.

"We got a runner on the sixth floor. He took the ice gem, and he's still on the loose. We believe he's somewhere on the first floor," one of the agents said over the walkie talkie. I reached for my walkie talkie and pulled it toward my face.

"Leave that kid to me. I'll handle it," I replied.

"Yes sir," he replied. I hooked the walkie talkie back onto my belt and stared at the man lying on the ground.

"Take care of him," I said to the agent next to me.

"Yes sir," he replied as I began to walk out of the room. I stopped for a second before I left the room and quickly turned around.

"I hope you know that your friends along with the ice gem are now...mine. And that's a promise," I told Charlie. He looked at me in fear as I began my search for the boy with the ice gem.

Chapter Thirty-Eight

LIAM SCARR

I bolted down the staircase. I had only gone down one floor, and I heard multiple gunshots coming from a few floors down. I looked down, and I quickly saw that a number of security agents were sprinting up the stairs. They were only about two floors under me. I was forced to stop on the eighth floor as I was clueless as to what I should do now.

"Charlie, I can't make it to the third floor. I'm compromised on the eighth floor as it is," I said over my walkie talkie.

"There's almost a hundred agents stationed on the first floor. I can't even leave the control room," he replied. I moved into one of the labs on the eighth floor that was directly below the tenth-floor lab we broke into. I looked out the window, and the ladder was right next to it. I made sure to first lock the door and barricade it with one of the large tables. There were still agents outside the back of the building but only about five.

"Rick, you're no longer a lookout. Help me take out the five agents surrounding the ladder," I said.

"Great. I've been waiting for some action," he replied. I

watched him jump out of the van as he began to unload on the agents. He was able to kill two of them within seconds. I pulled the window up, and I shot them from above. Bullets flew toward the Blue Mystique and the eighth-floor window, but the agents were pinned in the middle of the back parking lot with nowhere to hide. I gunned down one of them while Rick took out the other two. I heard the banging of multiple footsteps on the eighth floor, so I knew I needed to move quickly.

"Rick, cover me!" I said through the walkie talkie as I hopped out the window. I rapidly made my way down the ladder.

Bang! Bang!

Rick shot one of the agents, and he free fell from the eighth floor. I was forced to hang onto the far right side of the ladder. I had only one hand on the metal ladder, and it almost slipped off. I swung myself back onto the center as I continued to crawl down. Rick continued to fire shots at the agents who were still in the eighth-floor window. Five. Four. Three. Two and one. I hopped onto the hard concrete ground, and I sprinted to the van. Luckily, I didn't have to sprint very far out in the open. I was able to make it behind the tall thick trees covering the van. Rick and I put our guns away and jumped into the van.

There were still bullets coming at us, but the Blue Mystique is bulletproof. Rick started the van, and he whipped out of the parking lot next to the POE Labs and onto the street.

"Where are the others?" Rick asked.

"Jack's on a little suicide mission looking for Ava and this Paul guy, and it seems like Charlie is trapped on the first floor," I replied.

"So what's our next move boss?" Rick asked eagerly. I sighed as I quickly determined our options. Rick had already pulled the van onto the street, and we were about to be on our way. I had no response for him.

"Should we leave them behind?" Rick asked.

"Yeah, let's get outta here," I told him. He continued driving away from the POE Labs, and I started to get a weird feeling in my head.

"Scarr," a woman's voice whispered. I jumped, and Rick looked at me weirdly.

"What is it boss?" he asked.

"Do you hear that?" I asked.

"Scarr," the woman's voice whispered again. I thought it could be Ava, but I didn't recognize the voice at all.

"That. That. You didn't hear that?" I asked alarmed.

"I didn't hear anything," he replied. I got a weird feeling in my head. For some reason, I felt a sudden urge that Rick and I should go back. But not for Charlie and not for Ava. But for Jack Colson. I tried to focus as I knew my money-driven criminal mind would never actually come up with such an idiotic idea.

"Someone's in my head," I quietly said to myself so Rick couldn't hear me. I looked around trying to figure out what was going on, but I came up with no explanation.

"Jack needs you," the voice whispered. I closed my eyes, and I felt like I sunk into my seat. I fell a hundred feet from the sky landing on my feet in some cave. The cave was dark, and I couldn't see anything. A small light flickered above me, and I jumped. I pulled out my gun and blindly fired two shots into the darkness.

"I'm a fan of games, but not this one!" I screamed. I looked around, but there was no one. There was a quiet cricket chirp that made the cave not completely silent.

"Show yourself!" I screamed. I began to walk into the darkness, and my vision started to become more and more impaired.

"I killed tons of people. I'm not afraid to add another one to the list!"

I walked far enough where I couldn't even see my hand if it was right in front of my face. I was lost in the darkness.

"You're more than just a criminal," a voice said in the distance.

"No, actually I'm not," I replied.

"How do you explain your last assignment for the S.O.A.S. then?" she replied. I took a deep breath and fired two more shots into the darkness before my gun disintegrated into dust.

"As I told Austen Wolfe, Bethany Anderson had an abusive husband, and it wasn't my choice to decide if they should get married whether he thought so or not. She clearly needed some help. Are you going to show yourself or what?" I yelled at the voice.

"Jack needs help, too," she said loudly.

"It's different," I replied.

"Not as much as you think," she replied as I felt a hand rest on my shoulder. I turned around, and Rick was tapping me on the shoulder.

"Boss. This is no time to be sleeping," Rick said. I looked around in confusion. I could still see the POE Labs through the back window of the van in the distance.

"Turn the car around," I said.

"What?" Rick replied angrily.

"I know what it sounds like, but I have a plan. Trust me. Just do it," I told him.

"Alright boss," he replied. He uncontrollably whipped a U-turn and the van fishtailed to the right which almost made us flip. The car crashed back down on its four legs as it sprinted as fast as possible back to the POE Labs.

CHAPTER THIRTY-NINE
JACK COLSON

I continued crawling through the narrow air vent. The metal was cold around me, and I started to run out of room. I attempted to move fast, but it wasn't going well. I continued on and came across a drop in the air vent. There was nowhere to go except down.

"Ava, where should I go? I can't turn around." As soon as I said that I heard the agents' uniforms rubbing against the metal air vent walls.

"Jump down the air vent," she replied. I looked over my shoulder, but I still couldn't see the agents. I looked down, and it was practically straight down. I took Ava out of my pocket, and she was able to create a metal block behind me which temporarily occupied the agents. I dove down the air vent and broke right through the end of it. I ended up landing on a concrete floor under the vent. I landed directly on my back, and I was certainly in some pain. I was in a dark room and couldn't see anything around me. I stood up, and I held Ava in the air as a light.

"Where are we?" I asked.

"I think we are in some sort of basement," she replied. I looked around the room and attempted to feel around for a light switch. After a minute, I found the switch and flicked it on. There was an elevator to my right and a door on the other wall behind me. The room was empty with concrete walls. I slowly walked toward the door, and I flicked the lights on.

"Paul," I said loudly as I noticed he was locked up in a cell in front of me. The cell was small with only a bed and a toilet inside of it. Paul was sitting on the foot of his bed and stood up immediately when he saw me.

"What are you doing here?" he asked surprised to see me.

"We came to break you out. We're here to save you," I said as I ran up to the cell.

"Jack, this is a bad idea. You'll be captured," he replied clearly in fear.

"Not if we go quickly. Do you know where the key is?" I asked.

"We don't need a key. Point me toward the cell...and Paul?" Ava said.

"What is it?" he asked.

"You should stand back," she replied. Ava froze the jail bars into ice. The jail bars turned to icicles, and Paul was able to easily break them with his foot.

"Now let's get out of here before we all get captured,"

Paul said. We ran toward the elevator, and I hit the first-floor button.

"I think you should take this," I said to Paul as I handed him the pistol Liam gave me earlier.

"Perhaps that's a wise decision, but the ice gem's abilities are significantly more vital for aiding our escape. It's far more superior than a gun with some bullets," he replied more calmly than before.

The elevator doors slid open, and we were right back by the staircase I came out of before. However, this time there were at least fifteen agents surrounding us. Half of them stood on each side of us. I noticed that the main doors behind half the agents had been blown to pieces. The floor was basically glass with all the pieces from the main doors covering the floor. I turned to my left, and a middle-aged gentleman dressed in a black suit with a red button-down shirt underneath was there to greet us.

"Wolfe," Paul whispered.

"Well, if it isn't the man of the hour, Mr. Jack Colson. You know, you've gone through a lot of trouble these past few days. Honestly, you managed to keep Ava out of my hands longer than I expected, after I determined her whereabouts of course. I'm sorry that our introduction had to come at such a tragic moment. You overlooked the fact that someone of my power and wealth would eventually be able to track the location of the ice gem. You didn't think of that at all did you?" Wolfe said.

"You're not getting Ava no matter what you think! I won't let you!" I screamed.

"I just took care of your friend Charlie, and I think you're next on the list," Wolfe said. I was speechless for a few seconds before I held out the ice gem toward him. However, he held his gold revolver in the air, so I didn't attempt to freeze him.

"Your gun won't stand a chance against the ice gem," I said.

"Clearly the old man hasn't told you everything you need to know about the Power of Four. Luckily, I'm here to inform you before you make a deadly mistake," Wolfe replied.

"What's he talking about?" I asked Paul.

"He's already destroyed the red stone and the earth stone, and when that happened, the abilities from the stones were passed onto him, which he was able to transfer into his gold revolver," Paul replied.

"That's right. All these abilities are harnessed in one handheld revolver. So why don't you hand over the ice gem before I have to burn you to ash and take it by force?" he said powerfully.

"It's alright Jack. I'll be okay," Ava said.

I heard a humming sound coming in the distance. I didn't

know what it was, but it continually kept getting louder and louder. The security force blocked my view of the road, but I heard a car slam on its brakes right near the POE Labs.

"Hand it over now!" Wolfe commanded.

"Someone need a lift?" Rick yelled.

I immediately looked toward the street, and the Blue Mystique came flying through where the POE Labs entrance used to be. I jumped on the ground in the direction of the back door. Wolfe and the remaining agents to my left began running away from the van as the other half of the security agents were thrown back ten feet. Rick drove directly into them. Liam slid the van door open as he and Rick began to fire at them.

"Get the kid! Don't let them escape!" Wolfe screamed.

"Kid, let's go now!" Liam yelled at me.

Ava was able to freeze two of the agents. Wolfe wasn't able to get close enough to get a good shot with the gold revolver with all the gunfire in the room. Paul was on the ground near the elevator, and I signaled for him to follow me toward the van. Liam and Rick took out half the force, shooting at them before the remaining agents were forced to fall back. Wolfe attempted to use the revolver against us, but he was too late. We all hopped in the Blue Mystique, and Rick quickly drove out of the building.

"Strap yourselves in back there," Rick said. I looked through the back window and I saw two black Escalades pull out from the POE Labs.

"That was fast," I said.

"Yeah, we'll have to take them out. We may have to start off roading in a minute," Liam replied.

"I got that covered," Rick said.

"I don't think this is the safest strategy," Paul said.

"Well, I'm not a law-abiding citizen. I don't do things that are safe grandpa," Liam replied vainly.

There were no buildings on either side of us, so Rick took a hard right off the road. We were driving on the grass now, and the cars followed in our tracks. Liam pulled down his window as he began to fire a few shots their way. The shots failed to do any significant damage to the cars.

"Open the sunroof," I said.

"What are you thinking?" Paul asked nervously.

"Alright kid," Liam said as the sunroof slowly opened.

"Come on Ava. This is all you," I told her. I poked my head out of the sunroof and pointed the ice gem at one of the cars. A bolt of cold air shot out of Ava freezing one of the Escalades in seconds. I ducked back down to avoid the gunshots that were coming from the other car.

"Nice shot," Paul said.

"I'll get the last one," I replied. I didn't want to risk getting shot so I just poked Ava out of the sunroof. I aimed her in the direction of the other car and my arm kicked back.

"Aaaaaaah!" Ava screamed. I immediately pulled her back into the van and her crystals were flashing on and off quickly.

"Ava...Ava. What's happening?" I screamed.

"The S.O.A.S. has a particular gun that is able to temporarily neutralize Ava for a short amount of time. She'll be alright in about an hour," Paul replied.

"Well, that's good news for her, but we don't have an hour," Liam said.

"The van can only withstand so many gunshots," Rick replied. Liam pulled down his window, and he began firing more shots at the car.

"I can't get a clear shot from here," Liam yelled. Rick continued going over bumps and swerving on the grass. He weaved back onto the road, and Liam attempted to fire some shots, but none of them were able to do any damage.

"Hold on!" Rick screamed as he switched the van into sport mode as we were able to create a more comfortable gap between us and the Escalade.

"Will this van hold together with all these bullets coming at us?" Paul asked.

"Let's hope so, or this escape will be for nothing," Liam

replied. I grabbed one of the rifles in the back and quickly loaded it up.

"What do you plan to do with that?" Paul asked.

"I'm going to hit the bird. I have the feel. I'm confident about it," I said. I poked my head out of the sunroof and quickly aimed. I fired one shot, two shots, and one more.

Bang!

The third bullet soared straight through the front left tire. The car quickly lost control as it swerved back and forth before flipping on its side off the road.

"Hahahaha!" everyone screamed in joy as the last car was taken out. I ducked back down in the car, and Paul patted me on the back.

"You did it, Jack. You did it!" he said, smiling at me.

"I know," I replied laughing. Rick continued to drive down the street, but now he wasn't trying to escape two S.O.A.S. vehicles. Now, he was just trying to make it to the last stop—Caesars Palace in Las Vegas.

CHAPTER FORTY

JACK COLSON

After the dreadful ride that lasted an eternity, we finally arrived in Las Vegas. The sun was down, and the city was lit up with millions of lights. There was nobody on the streets since they were all packed in the casinos that covered the block.

"I never did thank you guys for coming back for me," I said.

"Yeah, if it wasn't for Scarr hearing voices and taking a quick nap we would have been on our way," Rick said

"Voices? Were you pulled into a dream?" Paul asked.

"Probably was," Rick replied.

"That's enough Rick. I wasn't pulled into anything. You can take your mystical beliefs somewhere else old man. I came back for my money, and once I get it, Rick and I will be on our way," Liam blustered.

"Where are these Stone Rescuers anyway?" Rick asked.

"It's Stone Saviors, and there's a small passageway in the lobby of Caesars Palace which leads to their hideout," Paul replied.

Rick pulled the van directly in front of the Caesars Palace. The hotel was humongous. It looked like it was a hundred floors. Paul, Liam, Rick, and I all walked into the hotel lobby. It was gorgeous. Large round lights hung from the ceiling while the walls were covered with rare paintings and amazing architectural designs. The floor also contained similar designs to the walls, and in the middle of the lobby was a statue of two women with a fountain surrounding them.

"How do we know where the hideout is? It could be anywhere in this gigantic building," I said.

"Follow me. I know where the entrance is," Paul replied.

We slowly walked past the lobby making sure not to draw any unnecessary attention to ourselves. We made it to a wide hallway where we stopped at a door that read *Do Not Enter*.

"The Stone Saviors' hideout is through this door. I've been here before," Paul said.

"It better be. I want my money," Rick mumbled as he got up in Paul's face.

"You'll get your money," Ava screamed from my pocket.

I opened the door, and it seemed like we entered another dimension.

The hideout was a small room, but there were still upwards of thirty people crowded into it. At the bottom of a staircase, there was a large round table in the middle of the room, and maps covered the walls. Many locations on the walls had red dots with writing next to them. There was a picture of all four of the stones on the wall. The ice gem, the red stone, the earth stone, and the death stone. Most of the people in the room wore nice gray pants accompanied by a short sleeve button-down gray shirt with a symbol on the left part of their chest like a polo shirt. The symbol was a circle where each of the four colors made up twenty five percent of the line color. The colors were blue, red, green, and black which clearly represented the four stones. Outside of the many people that wore the gray uniforms, there were five people that wore different colors than the rest of the crowd. There were three women and two men dressed in different colored shirts than the rest of the people. One of the men wore a green collared shirt while the other man wore a red collared shirt. Similarly, one of the women wore a blue collared shirt while the other woman wore a black collared shirt. However, the last woman was dressed in all white. She wore tight white pants and a white tank top with a white sports jacket over it. The five people dressed in multicolors all sat in chairs around a large round table while the others in gray were on computers and examining the maps around the room.

Everyone in the room quickly laid eyes on us. The people in gray immediately turned to the five people sitting at the round table for answers, but they didn't say anything. Paul stopped, so Liam, Rick, and I all waited behind him. I noticed that the people dressed in multicolors were all whispering to each other. The room was completely silent until the woman in the white stood up from her chair.

"It's good to have you back Paul," the woman said.

"It's a pleasure, your highness," he replied as he took a bow. We looked at him awkwardly as Rick, Liam, and I were not aware that we were meeting royalty of some sort.

"Who are these strangers you have brought before us?" she asked.

"These are some of my friends. They rescued me from Austen Wolfe's capture. The boy had come across one of our stones in Bermuda," he replied. The people in gray quickly turned to us, and their facial expressions were a mix of happiness and amazement. The woman looked at me as she waited to see the stone. I reached into my pocket and held Ava in the air.

"Truly wonderful to see you again, Ava," she said smiling.

"It's nice to see you again, too," Ava replied.

"I thought you were thriving in Bermuda. However, we witnessed the energy count dramatically rise a few days ago. We came looking for you, but we were unable to find you. Why did you reveal yourself?" she asked.

"I called out to Jack. His energy count was significantly higher than that of a normal person. I thought that he could help me. He was going to be killed, and I couldn't let that happen," Ava said dramatically.

"I see," she replied. She looked at me closely. She pushed her chair out as she began to walk toward me. She stood at the bottom of the staircase that we were standing on and signaled for me to come forward. I slowly walked down to her until I reached the end of the staircase. She held her hands out, and I placed Ava on them.

"If Ava saw something in you, then you are welcome here," she said.

"Thank you miss-"

"Katz. Irene Katz, but Irene is just fine," she replied cutting me off.

"It's a pleasure to meet you. My name is Jack Colson," I said.

"A pleasure to meet you, too," she replied.

"I also promised that the other two men accompanying Paul, Jack, and I would receive a reward of 200,000 dollars for their courageous act of helping us rescue Paul. They also helped bring me to Caesars Palace all the way from Brookfield," Ava said.

"Of course. They will be well rewarded," Irene replied as I saw Liam smile at me from the top of the staircase.

JACK COLSON

Irene placed a large suitcase on the round table in the center of the room. She unzipped it and revealed the 200,000 dollars inside.

"Mr. Scarr and Mr. Nelson, thank you for all your help," Irene said.

"You're just lucky I wanted my money. Otherwise, things would have turned out very differently," Liam said.

"Despite your indignant remarks Mr. Scarr, the actions I witnessed with my own eyes were truly heroic, no matter what you believe," Paul replied. Liam ignored Paul's comment as he just looked at him in silence without any emotion.

"Rick, take the money to the van," Liam said as he walked outside the Stone Saviors' hideout followed by Rick. I ran out of the lobby and followed them to the Blue Mystique. Rick was placing the money in the back of the van while Liam waited for him. They looked over at me confused as I stood at the lobby entrance.

"What is it kid? You didn't get to say a proper goodbye?" Liam said sarcastically.

"I thought you were planning on staying," I said.

"Well, I'd rather leave. If I stay, it's a death wish, and I'm planning on robbing a few more banks before that day comes," Liam replied.

"As do I," Rick added.

"How can you just leave? In the past few days, you've had half of your crew wiped out, and it seems like you don't even care-"

"It's not my problem," Liam replied, interrupting me.

"So you're just taking your money and leaving? I haven't even seen you shed one tear for your crew members' deaths. I'm trying to hold it together. Look what happened to Brian!" I shouted. My nose was sniffling, and a few teardrops began to run down my face. I quickly wiped them away.

"Not one tear!" I shouted at them.

"I'm not sentimental," Liam replied emotionless.

"How can you be so selfish?" I shouted. The people in the parking lot looked at me weirdly now that I was screaming at the top of my lungs. More tears began to drip down my face as I kept thinking about what Brian must've gone through.

"Do you even feel sorry for them?" I shouted. We stared at each other in silence. Tears continued to pour down my face like my eyes were faucets while Liam stood there with a straight face.

"Do you?" I shouted. His face got so close to mine, they were almost touching.

"There are only two things I care about in this world: myself and money...does that answer your question?" he blustered as he turned around and opened the door of the van. Liam shut the door as Rick came out of the van.

"Rick," I said.

"Yeah kid," he mumbled in his deep voice. I reached into my pocket and handed him an envelope.

"Can you give this to Liam for me once you get home or wherever you're going?" I said. He examined the envelope as he flipped it over to see if there was anything written on it.

"What is it?" he asked.

"A letter" I replied.

"Mmhmm," he mumbled as he stuffed the envelope in his pocket, closed the back door, and hopped back into the van. The van started up, and I watched Liam and Rick drive out of the parking lot of Caesars Palace.

I turned away and walked back inside and through the lobby, all the way to the door that read *Do Not Enter*. I entered the Stone Saviors' hideout. Everyone had remained in the same spots they were before. Paul immediately came over to me, and we quickly left the hideout and headed to the roof of the building. We could see the entire city from where we were.

"What's the matter, Jack?" Paul asked.

"Liam and Rick just left. I know they're criminals, but Liam came back for me. For us. He saved us. How could he just leave like that?" I asked sadly.

"You can't expect so much from everyone, especially people like them. They're master thieves, not heroes," he replied.

"But they saved us. Didn't they?" I asked as I sat down on the concrete roof.

"I was meaning to talk to you about that. I only briefly met Mr. Scarr and Mr. Nelson, so I may not know for sure, but I believe there's something more about why they saved us," he said as he sat down next to me.

"What do you mean?" I asked.

"Huh, I didn't tell you my full story when we first met—specifically what happened after I hid Ava in Bermuda.

"I originally told you that I went into hiding back in my cabin in Brookfield, however, Irene Katz and the rest of the Stone Saviors leaders showed up at my doorstep. They agreed that they would protect me and Ava, too. I told them where I hid Ava, and we brought her here to Caesars Palace. I became a Stone Savior. My job was to protect the stones at all costs.

"By time, the Stone Saviors were already devastated that the Earth God Shane had been killed weeks before, and the earth stone had been destroyed by Austen Wolfe. I met the other two Farisphonites though. I already knew the Ice Queen Ava, who was the oldest of the Farisphonites by decades. The King of Fire, Max, was around my age. He was the conscience of the red stone. I met the final Farisphonite years later. She was a late bloomer as she was only six years old when the Stone Saviors took her in. Miya Hart was her name. The Death Goddess. She was the only Farisphonite that opted not to be trapped in her stone. She decided to wield the stone rather than use the powers from the inside.

"For years, I fought beside them putting my life on the line. Until one day in 2010, we got an encrypted code from Irene Katz telling us that we must meet the Stone Saviors at the Diamond Head Volcano at midnight. I thought it was strange that she would ask this of us since we were on a voyage in search of any remains of the earth stone after the explosion. We hoped to find all the pieces all over the globe, but we couldn't find more than two.

"We met at the Diamond Head Volcano...where Austen Wolfe had set a trap. He had a hundred security agents surrounding us, and we were forced to turn over the red stone to him. He threw it into the lava, which released Max from the red stone. His men quickly gunned him down despite the fact that he attempted to use his powers. He wasn't able to kill them all; there were just too many of them. He killed the rest of the Stone Saviors that accompanied me on our voyage. He shot me twice. Once in the shoulder and once in the leg. I barely survived...but I had failed. After that, Miya Hart disappeared at the early age of ten. I then decided that I should retire and live out the rest of my life in Brookfield apart from all the Stone Saviors," he said.

"Wow, I'm sorry," I replied.

"Although that is a tragic story, I know you wanted to know how the King of Fire was killed," he said.

"How does this relate to Liam saving us?" I asked.

"Have you ever heard of the dormant mind Jack?" he asked.

"I don't think so," I replied.

"The dormant mind is the piece of your brain that you don't have access to. Some people are able to reach back and pull an idea or two from their dormant mind, but it would take a certain event or a person to be able to awaken it for you. The Farisphonites have a unique ability that allows them to awaken the dormant mind temporarily. The Death Goddess Miya Hart even at an extremely young age had great success unleashing people's dormant minds. I believe that Miya Hart has revealed herself for the first time in ten years. I think that she realized that Ava and you were in trouble, and she was able to access Mr. Scarr's dormant mind through a dream. I think that Miya Hart revealed a deep interior thought of his which allowed him to have a change of heart and come back to save us. If my theory is right, then you should go with Irene Katz to Ruby Falls in Tennessee. It's an underground limestone cave. If she realizes the threat of Austen Wolfe and the energy connection between you and Ava, then she will call out to you and reveal herself," Paul said.

"So you think Miya Hart tampered with Scarr's mind so that he would save us?" I said.

"Yes, I do," he replied as we both stood up and headed back downstairs toward the hideout.

CHAPTER FORTY-TWO

AVA

Ten years ago...

The Council of Gemology sat around the circular table in the center of the Stone Saviors' hideout. They were all in silence until the red stone representative Hagan cleared his throat.

"Miya Hart is gone. Paul has just gone into hibernation, and the King of Fire, Max, is deceased. This is madness. What do you suggest we do?" Hagan shouted.

"The rise of Austen Wolfe has come, and now Ava is the only stone that remains in our possession," Libitina said.

"There's nothing we can do," Crystal added.

"So you suggest we just sit here and wait for Austen Wolfe to find the death stone? Why don't we go out and find Miya before she gets herself killed?" Hagan almost panicked.

"We won't find Miya if she doesn't want to be found," Libitina replied.

"How can you be so sure?" Hagan asked angrily.

"Because she knows. She is the death stone representative. It's her job to know. Miya Hart won't be found if she doesn't want to be. She's an independent girl. She does things differently than the other Farisphonites. We won't find her. I suggest that Ava go into hiding as well," Irene stated. The council members all stared at Irene in silence. I could feel the anger coming off of Hagan. He was fuming with rage.

"Are you mad?" Hagan replied. Crystal, Libitina, and Terran were deer in the headlights as their eyes were wide open. Even I was amazed that Hagan would reply with such a rude comment to the leader of the Council of Gemology. Irene looked at him surprised.

"I know you're feeling the effects of Max's death right now. We are all upset. It was unexpected, and we couldn't have prepared for that," Irene said.

Hagan placed his head on the table as he attempted to hide his face. I heard him sniffle a few times. He lifted up his head, and the heat of his anger cooled from the tears that flowed down his cheeks. He quickly stood up and sprinted out of the hideout. Irene grabbed me off the table, and she held me in the air.

"Hagan is obviously emotional, so we will continue this meeting without him. Crystal, do you think that Ava should go into hiding?" Irene Katz asked.

"I think we should do whatever it takes to protect Ava, and if you believe that Ava should be hidden away from the Stone

Savior hideout, then that is what we shall do," Crystal replied.

"I believe that Bermuda will be a good place for me to hide. It has an elaborate system of caves. I feel it will be difficult for Austen Wolfe to track me if I avoid using my powers in an area where I'm hidden within a series of rock formations that have been there for millions of years," I said.

"That is a great idea Ava. Everyone in favor of this plan say 'Aye,'" Irene said.

"Aye," they all replied.

"Great, we are all in favor. Ava will go into hiding, and we will monitor her. If Ava is faced with any trouble, then we will all come to her assistance if needed," Irene stated.

"Ava, if you need us, you know where to find us," Irene said.

"I know," I replied.

"Austen Wolfe will not achieve the power of four. Not on my watch," Irene said as the Council all stood up and dispersed throughout the hideout.

Chapter Forty-Three

Jack Colson

We walked into the Stone Saviors' hideout, and the group of people sitting at the round table in the center of the room stared at us.

"Irene has to introduce you to some important people," Paul whispered in my ear. Irene quickly stood up as she signaled for me to come toward her.

"Jack, I'd like to introduce you to the Council of Gemology which is the Board of Directors for the Stone Saviors. Terran is the representative for the earth stone, Crystal is the representative of the ice gem, Hagan is the representative of the red stone, and Libitina is the representative of the death stone. Their shirts correspond to the color of the stone they represent. I am the Chairman of the Council of Gemology, and our job is to protect the stones at all costs. We honor the sacrifice you made to protect Ava, and I assure you that we will keep Ava safe," she said.

"I did what I could to protect her. I wasn't going to let her be taken by Austen Wolfe," I replied. Irene chuckled as she looked around at the rest of the council members.

"I believe that there is more to that story than you say. Ava has discussed your energy count before. I think that you don't understand your importance. Not yet. Paul has told me about his hypothesis that Miya Hart has revealed herself to your friend Liam Scarr. He suggested that we travel to Ruby Falls in Tennessee. If he is right, then Miya Hart will be able to return here so that the remaining Farisphonites can be back together again. She'll also be able to help you discover your abilities."

"My abilities?" I asked surprised. I looked at Paul confused, but he didn't say anything.

"Ava said that you successfully wielded the ice gem on multiple occasions. Only people with the N plus bloodline would have the ability to successfully control it. Miya Hart may be able to help you tap into your abilities" she replied.

"Wow, that's...How come I have the N plus bloodline?" I asked. Irene looked toward Paul and then back at the other council members.

"We aren't entirely sure. We don't know how it's possible," she said. I stood there in silence confused. I didn't know what to think.

"Why me?" I asked myself. I had already traveled all this way protecting Ava, but I had not realized how far I had come.

A few of the Stone Saviors packed a few bags into a white

Porsche. The car looked new as there was not a scratch on it. The tires were shiny, and the windows were tinted. I stood on the sidewalk as I waited for the car to be packed. I felt a light tap on my left shoulder, and I saw Paul was standing behind me.

"I don't know if I'm ready for this," I said.

"Ready for what?" Paul asked calmly.

"At first I just wanted more. I wanted more in my life than just school. I saw an opportunity to be more than just a high school student. To be a hero."

"And you are," Paul replied, interrupting me.

"I may have saved Ava, but I'm scared. I want to help Ava. I do. I don't want Ava to be taken by Austen Wolfe, and now that I have these abilities….It's just a lot to take in. I feel like there's loads of pressure on me. I'm persistent, but I'm not that smart. I'm not smarter than Austen Wolfe, and I'm not more powerful than he is either," I replied nervously.

"Nobody's perfect. You can only do so much. Everything will work out. Trust me Jack," he replied.

"Why aren't you coming with us to Ruby Falls? I need your guidance. I can't do this without you," I told him. He sighed as he patted me on the back.

"My years with the Stone Saviors are in the past. I'm too old and weak to fight alongside you," he said sadly.

"Where will you go? What if I need your help?" I asked nervously.

"I found a small place. It's a nice little cabin outside of Brookfield. Similar to my old place. If you need me, I'll be there. However, you should not need my help. Your training may not have been complete, but your courageous acts of saving both Ava and I from the POE Labs show that you have all the skills you need," he replied.

I nodded as I turned to look toward the car. Irene was sitting in the front seat, and the engine roared like a lion as she twisted the key. Paul and I stood on the sidewalk and watched as smoke ran out of the exhaust. Her window slowly rolled down until you couldn't see it anymore.

"Jack, let's go. The sooner we get there, the sooner we can bring Miya back," she said.

I looked at Paul as I thrust myself forward into his arms. I grabbed him tightly, and I didn't want to let go. His hands pressed against my upper back as he pulled me toward him.

"Okay Jack. Let's not keep Irene waiting," he said as his arms slowly returned to his side. I let go of him, and I quickly stood up straight like a statue. I looked both ways. In one direction was the past: Paul, the Stone Saviors, and my impulsive courage that led me to Las Vegas. In the other direction was what is yet to come. The future. The Farisphonite Miya

Hart who is responsible for protecting the death stone and stopping the S.O.A.S.

"Go on," Paul said.

I stood there in silence. My hands trembled as I had already dug myself a large hole. I was in too deep. Irene stared at me as she held Ava in her hand. I know I wanted more than just school in my life, but this was risky. Tons of the stunts I pulled the last few days were extremely dangerous. Austen Wolfe had seen my face. He knows who I am. There's a price on my head, and the question was did I want to risk my life to protect Ava?

"Do I want to be a hero? What if I don't succeed? Can I stop Austen Wolfe from achieving the Power of Four?" I asked myself. The wind combed my long brown hair in all different directions.

"There's nothing to be afraid of Jack. You're a hero and so much more," Paul said. I didn't even turn around to acknowledge his comment. I knew what I needed to do. I flung open the passenger door to the Porsche and sat down. The window was still open, and I saw Paul waving to me.

"We'll see each other soon. I promise," he shouted in his calming voice. I laid back in my chair and closed my eyes.

"To Ruby Falls," Irene said as the white Porsche drove out of the parking lot and sped up once it reached the empty Vegas streets.

CHAPTER FORTY-FOUR

JACK COLSON

We walked down a walkway under a shallow, arc-shaped entrance. A small brown sign read *Enter Here* in white letters above us while a garland formed the shape of a smile on the castle-like structure. The place was built of stone, and the square blocks were separated with crenels. I followed Irene into an elevator inside. The clear elevator doors slid closed, and I looked at the large rock that remained an inch from the door until we reached the cave. The doors slid open, and there was a curvy narrow pathway surrounded by large stones. There were weak lights attached to the stones along with lanterns hanging from the stone walls. The cave was dark and cold with stone jutting from the walls. I looked around and accidentally walked directly into one of the stones.

"Watch out. There are more stones positioned just like that," Irene said.

She pulled Ava out from her pocket and used her glowing blue crystal as a flashlight. There were spiders crawling on the low ceiling and webs on some of the rocks. We passed a television attached to one of the rocks. It was the late afternoon, so there were no tour guides here or anyone at all. The pathways began to decrease in size, and the ceilings began to get lower. I had to duck down a little bit just so I wouldn't hit my head on the rock ceiling above me.

"Why would someone decide to hide down here?" I asked.

"She loved this place. It's like a home to her. This is where she discovered the death stone," Ava replied. We continued walking forward, and the rocks on the ceiling began to form an upside-down trench. Some of the rocks looked like icicles as they hung down from the ceiling.

"Do you think Miya Hart will show herself?" Ava asked.

"If she realizes she's in danger, then yes," Irene replied. We walked into a large area in the cave where we could see more humongous upside-down trenches that were at least 145 feet above us. I looked around in amazement, but I wasn't able to see everything because the cave was too dark. A purple LED light appeared above us revealing an enormous waterfall pouring water into a small pool in front of us. I was shocked. I had never seen anything like this before. The noise of the water spilling over a hundred feet hitting the pool was loud but calming.

"I don't see anyone around. Maybe she's not here," I said.

"She'll reveal herself. We just need to give her a sign," Irene replied.

"What kind of sign?" I asked. She walked toward me and

placed Ava in my hand.

"The waterfall. Ava needs to connect with the waterfall," she said. I looked at Ava silently as I walked around the pool to the side closest to the waterfall. There was a railing around the small pool that I used to thrust myself up on one of the rocks. I firmly gripped the railing as I stood close to the waterfall.

"She has to feel the water to go in it," Irene shouted from the other side of the pool.

"Are you sure this'll work?" I asked.

"Just try it," she replied.

I leaned forward and reached my hand toward the waterfall. I felt a few droplets of water hit my hand and shivered because the water was freezing. Ava began to glow as I held her in the center of the waterfall. I waited a minute, and I looked at Irene for answers. She didn't say anything, and neither did I. Nothing was happening.

"Ava, what's going on?" I asked as the waterfall began to turn light blue like Ava.

"I don't feel anything. I can't reach her," she replied.

"It's not working," I shouted. I watched Irene whisper to herself as a light bulb must've gone off in her head.

"She doesn't want Ava. She wants you," she shouted a few times.

"What do you mean?" I shouted back.

"Close your eyes," she shouted. I closed my eyes and listened to the sound of the water. I thought about connecting with this Miya Hart, but nothing happened. I remained still and silent, but there was no sign. I quickly opened my eyes, and nothing changed.

"It's not working. Nothing's happening," I shouted.

"Try it again, maybe she didn't hear you," Irene shouted back.

I closed my eyes again and attempted to only focus on my surroundings. The cold water hitting my hand along with the ice gem and the light blue color of the waterfall. Some droplets of water sprinkled on my cheeks, and I rubbed them with the sleeve of my blue collared shirt. I waited two minutes in silence until I couldn't take it anymore.

"I don't think she's coming!" I shouted as I opened my eyes. I looked around confused as I was standing on the edge of the waterfall that was above me. I turned around to step away from the edge, but I slipped.

"AAAAAAAH!" I screamed as I fell into the water. I hit the water, but surprisingly I continued to fall through the pool floor and landed on concrete ground. I also wasn't standing in any water, and my hair wasn't even wet. I looked up, and there was a see-through circular glass window that looked right into the pool in which I had just landed. In a matter of seconds, the glass window disappeared.

"Am I dreaming?" I asked myself. I looked around, and I was still in the cave but in a different area. It was extremely dark. I couldn't see my hand in front of my face.

"Hello?" I said nervously. There was no response.

"Ava...Irene...Is anyone there?" I shouted.

"Hello?" I said again. I looked around but there was nothing but stones and empty space.

Chapter Forty-Five

Liam Scarr

The warehouse was dark and cold. It was different from the last warehouse we stayed in because this one was right in the town of Brookfield rather than on the outskirts. I walked toward a brown couch in the center of the empty warehouse and sat down. There was a small brown wooden table in front of the couch upon which I rested my feet. The couch was comfortable, and I looked around at our new home. The ugly rectangular ceiling lights were dangling above me, and the concrete walls were naked. The only furniture in the room was the couch and the small table. Rick entered the warehouse through the large garage door to my right.

"How do you like it, Rick? Our new place?" I said.

"What's our plan now Scarr?" Rick asked.

"What do you mean? We got the money, the place, and we can continue where we left off," I said excitedly.

"Robbing banks?" he asked unenthusiastically.

"You know I thought you'd be more excited," I replied.

"What about Jack?" he asked.

"What about him?" I asked.

"What do you think he's doing now?" he replied.

"Why do you care?" I asked angrily.

"I want revenge on the S.O.A.S. They killed Charlie, and we could be next," he said.

"So let me guess. You want to swoop in and…take down a billion-dollar operation?" I replied sarcastically.

"I like to kill people, but I'd rather kill a bunch of wrongdoers as revenge rather than some innocent people at a bank," he said. I stood up and began to slowly walk toward him.

"Have it your way, but I'm not interested in being a hero," I blustered.

"That young girl Bethany who you saved from her abusive husband might think differently," he mumbled.

I reached into my holster and quickly pulled out my pistol. I pointed my gun at his head, but he slung his AK-47 over his shoulder into his arms. It was like a western standoff as we both stood there silently with our guns pointed at each other's heads.

"I thought I told you not to bring up that name," I blustered.

"Charlie was right. I think you want more than just a life of crime," he mumbled in his low voice. We stared at each other emotionless as we both lowered our weapons.

"Well, you thought wrong. I think you've just gone soft. What happened to the man that was going to take out Charlie once we got our money from the stone? And now…NOW, you want to save them? Rick. Rick. Rick. We may have lost a few members of our gang, but the Red Sinners gang will survive. I'm the brains, you're the muscle, Doug and Perk were our henchmen, Charlie was our tech guy, and Hank was our driver. They were loyal and served as vital members of the gang, but the truth is…they can be replaced, and so can you. Care for a little advice? Why don't you listen to the brains rather than your idiotic self!" I blustered.

Rick stared at me as if he was about to beat me into a million pieces. He breathed heavily, and I could almost feel his breath on me from ten feet away.

"I want my revenge," he replied angrily as he reached into his pocket and slapped a piece of paper on my chest. He held his hand there until I grabbed the paper out of his hand.

"Is this your pitch?" I asked snarkily. He ignored my comment as he stomped out of the large room like a dinosaur. I sat back down on the couch and rested my feet on the table. I ripped the envelope open and grabbed a letter out of it. I threw the envelope on the couch and began to read.

Dear Liam Scarr,

If you're reading this, then my prediction was wrong. You decided to leave Las Vegas after you received your money from the Stone Saviors. You're walking away from your friends. We need you, and you're turning your backs on us. I know you're a criminal, and I'm aware that money is extremely important to you, but I know that you want more than that. You went back for us. For me. For Paul. For Ava. You saved us, and I don't care what your motives were. You did. You may not admit it, but I believe that behind your snarky rough exterior is a sensitive heroic person. Your heroic personality will reveal itself eventually. It's only a matter of time.

Sincerely,

Jack Colson

"That resilient son of a bitch," I said to myself quietly.

I stared at the letter as I rubbed my chin. My eyes began to become misty, so I rubbed my knuckles on them. I shook my head as I attempted to not let my emotions get the best of me. I began to think about what Jack, Charlie, and Rick all said.

"Are they right? Am I more than just a criminal? Will my heroic personality reveal itself?" I asked myself. I reached for the letter and placed it back into the envelope. I buried it under the couch cushions as I stood up.

"Rick," I yelled.

"What is it boss?" he shouted from another part of the warehouse.

"It's time to leave," I replied loudly. I walked toward the Blue Mystique as I exited the warehouse.

"Well...it's only a matter of time," I said to myself.

CHAPTER FORTY-SIX

JACK COLSON

I held my hands out trying to feel my surroundings. I blindly walked around until I felt a large rock to my right. I grabbed onto the rock as I pulled myself toward the side of the cave. I slowly slid my body across the rock as I tried to find my way around. A light flickered on above me, which enabled me to see more clearly. The rock ceilings were low as I stood on the narrow pathway. There was dead silence...until I heard a faint noise in the distance. A chuckle.

"Hahahaha," a child's voice laughed faintly. I quickly moved toward the direction of the voice. The closer I moved to the laughter, the darker it got. The laughter quickly became louder and louder until I was once again surrounded by darkness.

"Miya?" I said nervously. The laughing immediately came to halt. Another light flicked on above me and hung down from a wire. The lightbulb dangled directly in front of my face. The light, however, was so weak I was only able to see about six feet in either direction.

"You're much calmer than your friend Liam Scarr," a

woman's voice said. I looked around confused, but I wasn't able to see anyone.

"I don't think he'd refer to us as friends," I replied sarcastically. There was no reply.

"Well, you're much more open with your feelings than he is. You are much easier to connect with," she said.

"I would hope so," I replied. I waited a minute for her reply, but she didn't say a word.

"Are you planning on showing yourself? I came here to help you," I shouted. I continued to look around, but there was still no one.

"I know you're here somewhere Miya. I'm not here to hurt you. There's nothing to be afraid of. The Stone Saviors have sent me to bring you back to Las Vegas where you will be safe," I said loudly.

I heard the sound of footsteps coming toward me. They continually got louder and louder until I saw two large black boots standing six feet in front of me. A woman around my age walked into the dim light and stood in front of me. She wore black tight jeans with a black belt. She also wore a sexy short black shirt which exposed her belly button. The shirt had four buttons coming down the front but one of them was undone. It almost looked like a tank top that was two sizes too small with thin straps over her shoulders. She wore a pearl white necklace around her neck that was incredibly beautiful. Her face was clear and looked as smooth as silk. She wasn't wearing any makeup, and her face shimmered in the dim light. She had long, black, wavy hair that reached the middle of her back. Most of her hair sat behind her shoulder but a few strands waved around her left eye making it difficult to see. Her eyes were wide open, and they matched the color of the ocean. Her light pink lips were open just enough that you could see her two front pearly white teeth.

"The Stone Saviors," she said.

"What?" I replied.

"You want me to return to Las Vegas," she said.

"Yes," I replied. She slowly nodded in response.

"I'm Jack Colson. I was told to come look for you. You're Miya Hart, the last remaining Farisphonites besides Ava," I said.

"I know," she replied.

"Paul Jankins told me to come and find you. He said that he believed that you revealed yourself to Liam Scarr," I said.

"I did it because I wanted him to save you. You're welcome by the way," she replied jokingly.

"I came here with Ava and Irene Katz. They want you to come back to them," I said eagerly.

"I may have helped your friend save you, but Austen Wolfe

is still very powerful and a threat to Ava and me," she said.

"Then teach me. I can help. I can help you defeat Austen Wolfe," I replied eagerly. She looked at me, disgusted by my eagerness.

"I wouldn't be so happy about this," she replied tersely.

"Why not?" I asked nervously.

"You do have powers...but it means there's a target on your back. That's why I was forced to hide out here," she said.

"Austen Wolfe already knows who I am. He's after me no matter what power I may possess. I'll do whatever I can to help Ava. I'm not afraid anymore. I'm not afraid of having powers. I'm not afraid of Austen Wolfe. I'm not afraid of the future."

"If I were you, I would be," she replied sharply. I looked at her confused. I tilted my head as I tried to comprehend what she meant by that.

"What do you mean?" I asked loudly but before I could finish, everything went white, and I was standing back on the rock holding Ava in the waterfall. I pulled the ice gem toward me as I jumped off the rock. I looked up and Irene was staring at the entrance to the cave. Miya slowly walked toward her as I watched from the other side of the pool.

"Miya," Ava said quietly.

"I'm coming back with you guys," Miya said with a little smirk on her face.

Chapter Forty-Seven

AUSTEN WOLFE

Men and women filled the S.O.A.S. headquarters dressed in suits and fancy dresses. It was the annual gala held each year to promote the S.O.A.S. socialistic policies and recruit new members. The large extravagant ballroom was packed with at least 300 people each holding a glass of champagne. They walked around as they took microscopic sips of their drinks and talked about subjects like the Dow Jones industrial average, real estate opportunities, vacation plans, and anything else that ran through the heads of wealthy business executives and politicians. I had to dress up in formal attire for the event, so I had on my finest tuxedo with a red cummerbund and matching red tie. My short hair was slicked back neatly, so I looked more presentable.

I stood by the edge of the table by myself until I noticed the Sweeney couple begin to approach me. I immediately lifted up my left arm as I hit the number one on my highly technological watch. The number one on the watch signaled to Ottron that I needed him right away, to pull me out of this conversation as soon as possible.

"Hi, Austen," they both said in sync. They looked extremely excited to see me, and I was disgusted by it. I rolled my eyes as I put on my fake nice attitude.

"Bob and Erica, it's great to see you again," I said as I shook both their hands. Bob was dressed in a goofy suit. His suit was sap green covered with a bunch of Christmas ornaments.

"How do you like my suit?" Bob asked foolishly. I wasn't going to tell him that he looked like a walking Christmas tree. He deserved to be shot showing up to a black-tie event wearing that outfit.

"It's very unique," I replied.

"He sewed it himself. He's so creative that way," Erica said laughing.

"Oh stop it, honey," he replied. I was inches away from pulling my gold revolver out of my jacket pocket and shooting Erica's Nanny McPhee-looking face. She was wearing a red fitted dress with a black fur collar. Luckily, she's very intelligent, or I wouldn't have any reason for having her in my organization. It infuriated me seeing Erica bringing her husband to these types of parties. He's dumber than Billy Madison.

"Mr. Wolfe, Ottron needs you in your office immediately," one of my security officers whispered in my ear. I sighed with relief.

"Yes, excuse me for just a moment," I said as I began to exit the ballroom.

"Bye," Bob replied.

"Toodle-loo," Erica added. I reached the tenth floor and walked down the hallway to my office. I opened the door and was astonished to see Liam Scarr sitting at my desk. His black shoes were resting on my desk as he was lounging back in my chair.

"At least one of us knows how to follow orders," he said sarcastically.

"What are you doing here?" I replied angrily.

"Ottron has had quite the day today," he said.

"What are you talking about?"

"He took a little trip with my partner Rick. Looks like you don't have a servant at your beck and call."

"You're bluffing," I said. I walked out of my office and scanned the hall.

"Ottron...Ottron!" I screamed. I heard a muffled voice behind me. I turned around, and Liam was standing up in front of me holding a handheld recording device in front of his chest. The muffled voice continued until finally, the words became clearer.

"Hello Ottron," Liam said.

"Afternoon Mr. Scarr," he replied.

"Where are you right now?"

"I am not able to determine my current location. There also appears to be a large man holding a gun at my head who claims he will split me into a thousand pieces."

"You're lucky I haven't done it yet, robot," Rick said.

Liam stopped the recording and placed it back in his pocket. I instantly pulled back my suit jacket as I grabbed my gold revolver and pointed it at Liam. He didn't even flinch. In fact, he didn't do anything. He just stared at me.

"You think you're so tough. I'm gonna kill you right now and find Ottron myself."

"If you plan on having all your secrets about the S.O.A.S. and the Power of Four revealed to the public, then by all means...do it," he said as I slowly lowered my weapon. "I didn't think so. Since Ottron contains memory files containing all of your personal files regarding the creation of the S.O.A.S. and your aspiration to achieve the Power of Four, it'd be very easy to upload them to the public."

"What do you want?"

"I want you to stay away from me, the kid, and the ice gem," he said as I stared at him in a fit of rage. "And these are clearly incriminating files, so I'll need a small compensation wired to a series of bank accounts to keep my mouth shut. Ten million dollars every year starting today should suffice," he said as

I chuckled.

"You're deranged if you think I'm accepting that ridiculous proposal," I replied. Liam walked around me and left the office.

"Where do you think you're going?" I screamed.

"I'm going to the bank to cash a check," he replied snarkily.

"You may get the money now, but don't count on this being an annual occurrence...I'll find a way to get Ottron back, and once I do you, and your friends will never be safe again!" I screamed as Liam entered the elevator. He turned around and looked back at me.

"It was a pleasure doing business with you," he replied rudely as the elevator doors closed. I walked back to my office angrily as I sat back in my chair.

Ring! Ring! Ring!

"Hello?" I said as I picked up the phone.

"Mr. Wolfe, we have Liam Scarr surrounded here in the lobby. What should we do with him?" one of the officers asked. I put my head down as I sighed in disbelief.

"Let him go," I said.

"What?"

"You heard me. I said let him go!" I said loudly.

"Yes boss," he replied.

I stood up in a fit of rage and threw the phone at the wall.

I looked out the window and saw Liam Scarr strutting down the street. How did I get bested by this degenerate, not once, but twice?

Chapter Forty-Eight

JACK COLSON

Two months later...

I walked into the Stone Saviors' hideout, and all eyes were on me. I walked toward the large round table in the middle of the room where all the members of the Council of Gemology were gathered. Irene stood up from her chair at the head of the table, and all the members stared at her intently. She stood erect with her fingers locked together in front of her chest.

"We honor your allegiance to the Stone Saviors, and we thank you for all you have had to endure to protect Ava as well as help us find Miya Hart. We have been fortunate enough to live the last two months without the threat of Austen Wolfe and the S.O.A.S. It is with great sorrow that I announce that Jack Colson will be leaving us. We wish you the best of luck on your journey and what lies ahead," she said.

I nodded, smiling as I looked at everyone around me.

"I wish you all the best," I replied. Irene walked toward me as she placed Ava in my hand. I grasped her hard in the palm of my hand. She was no longer cold like she once was. Or maybe I had just grown accustomed to the temperature.

"Goodbye, Jack," Ava said.

"Bye," I said softly as I handed Ava back to Irene. My hand felt wet as there were little water drops in my hand that resembled tears. I smiled sadly as I walked to the exit.

I was sitting in a small waiting room flipping through pages of the college brochure. I was one of the only people there since it was the summertime. I don't know many students who would willingly choose to be in a college at the end of August if classes haven't started yet. The only thing you'd be able to do is read books in the library, and frankly, that doesn't sound exciting.

"Mr. Colson, Mr. Ferris will see you now," a woman said. I stood up and followed her to a small office.

"Thank you," I replied as I sat down across from a man wearing a grey polo shirt with black pants. He had short brown hair, and I could see him looking up my name on his computer. He pulled up my file and looked at me.

"Mr. Colson, it's nice to meet you," he said.

"It's nice to meet you, too," I replied.

"I don't understand your situation. I talked with your guidance counselor, and he said that you had no desire to pursue your education until last week. He said you had not applied to any colleges, and you didn't intend to. You have a substantial amount of community service, but your grades are below the criteria we look for here at Ithaca College. Classes start in less than a week, and you're attempting to be enrolled in the class of 2024. I don't believe there is anything I can do to help you. Unless there is anything you would like to say, I think our meeting is just about finished," he said.

"I do have something to say....I-I know I didn't apply to any colleges. The reason I didn't was because I wasn't sure what I wanted to do in the future. I'm 18 years old and unlike other kids, I don't have my whole life planned out yet. I still don't. I have no idea what career path I want to pursue. I realize that I'm late to the game, and I know that my transcript shows that I don't have what it takes to be enrolled in this school. Over the summer I've been working with a man named Paul, and he told me that nobody's perfect and you can only do so much. I was always so terrified of failing. I created this illusion that I wasn't able to complete this summer mission that was handed to me. I was constantly seeking the help of others when in reality, everything I needed was there all along. It was me. I just didn't know it, and I promise you that I will do whatever it takes to be successful in this school. It's only a matter of time," I said confidently.

Sure enough, I was given that opportunity on a

probationary trial basis at Ithaca College.

A couple of days later, I moved into my dorm at the college. I quickly met some friends, and one night we decided to go out to a bar in Ithaca where I saw someone who had a familiar resemblance to Brian Shadow.

The bar was dimly lit, and the young man was sitting at the other end of the bar alone. I thought it couldn't be possible that my best friend was somehow still alive. Despite this, I walked over to the young man, and to my amazement it was him! I grabbed hold of Brian before he could see who it was. He turned around stunned and realizing who it was, gave me the biggest hug I had ever received.

I was so happy for Brian. He was attending Cornell as he had always dreamed of doing, and I was only a few minutes down the road.

About the Author

Michael Nyikos grew up in Westchester County, New York. He is presently a junior majoring in math at Union College in Schenectady, New York. From an early age, Michael has always had an insatiable fascination for all types of theatre, film, and the complex and detailed stories that draw one into the theatrical or cinematic experience. An avid sports enthusiast, Michael enjoys skiing, fishing, golfing, and playing lacrosse. He also can occasionally be found playing his guitar. Michael loves traveling and experiencing other cultures and cuisines as well. He has recently traveled to Spain, Portugal, Italy, Ireland, and France and looks forward to other adventures in the future.